STELLA RISING

STELLA RISING

Nancy Belgue

orca soundings

ORCA BOOK PUBLISHERS

Library and Archives Canada Cataloguing in Publication

Title: Stella rising / Nancy Belgue.
Names: Belgue, Nancy, 1951– author.
Series: Orca soundings.
Description: Series statement: Orca soundings

Identifiers: Canadiana (print) 20190168862 | Canadiana (ebook) 20190168870 |
ISBN 9781459825628 (softcover) | ISBN 9781459825635 (PDF) | ISBN
9781459825642 (EPUB)

Classification: LCC PS8553.E4427 S74 2020 | DDC jC813/.6—dc23

Library of Congress Control Number: 2019943952
Simultaneously published in Canada and the United States in 2020

Summary: In this high-interest novel for teen readers, sixteen-year-old
Stella is suddenly famous after her music video goes viral.

*Orca Book Publishers is committed to reducing the consumption
of nonrenewable resources in the making of our books. We make
every effort to use materials that support a sustainable future.*

Orca Book Publishers gratefully acknowledges the support for its
publishing programs provided by the following agencies: the Government of
Canada, the Canada Council for the Arts and the Province of British Columbia
through the BC Arts Council and the Book Publishing Tax Credit.

Edited by Tanya Trafford
Design by Ella Collier
Cover images by gettyimages.ca/Georgijevic (front) and
Shutterstock.com/Krasovski Dmitri (back)

ORCA BOOK PUBLISHERS
orcabook.com

Printed and bound in Canada.

23 22 21 20 • 4 3 2 1

To John, Daniel, Mike, Sarah and Tilly—the people who color my world.

Chapter One

"Oh no you didn't!" I stared at myself on the screen. I sounded like a leaf blower—loud, obnoxious and one-note. I covered my ears. I shut my eyes. I decided to throw myself out the window.

"Cut the drama," said Marnie, peeling my hands away from my ears. "You look amazing. And you sound great."

I opened one eye. I did look okay. Black T-shirt, holes in my jeans, black eyeliner strategically smudged. Then I heard myself stretching for the high note. "Oh god," I moaned. "Turn it off."

"You are so overreacting, Stell." Marnie hit *Pause* on the YouTube video.

"It's my worst nightmare. If I'd had any idea you were going to do this, I would never have let you record me."

"But Stell. The video is *awesome*."

Marnie is my oldest friend. Maybe my only friend. But she has lousy taste. No one could say I sounded anything but pathetic. "I sound pathetic."

"Look, you've had eight hundred views already," said Marnie. "In one hour!"

"And they are all laughing," I replied. "Or throwing up."

"Stop it. Just stop." Marnie scrolled down to the comments. "Listen to this:

'Who *is* this chick? She is killing it.' See? Throwing up? I don't think so."

"You're making that up," I said.

Marnie pointed her finger at the screen. "Nope. Here's another one. 'Better than the original!' Can you believe it?"

I shook my head. No, I couldn't believe it. But I still wanted it gone. All this attention was making my skin crawl. If there's one thing I know about social media, it's that when good comments lead, bad crap isn't far behind. The trolls would come out any second, and I didn't want to be around to read their horrible comments.

"Listen, I got to go. Viv's expecting me for dinner."

Marnie hooked her legs over the arm of the chair. "Seriously? You've got to be kidding me. Since when does your mom do dinner?"

"Since tonight." Marnie had a point though. Viv wasn't known for her cooking skills. To say the very least.

"Something's up. If she's making dinner for you, something is definitely up, kiddo."

"Maybe." There was no *maybe* about it. But I hated that Marnie was always right. "Anyway, I'm late." I wound my scarf three times around my neck, pulled on my black watch cap and shoved my feet into the battered pair of combat boots I'd found at Goodwill.

As I walked across the bridge, the wind took my breath away. Viv hated February, and my gut was telling me that it was only a matter of time until she took off. As I got nearer to the house, I could see that the lights were on in our basement apartment.

"Hey, Viv," I said as I let myself in. I'd been a latchkey kid since I was six, so I knew the drill. Viv's latest job was bartending at Whiskey Jack's, and we hardly ever saw each other. "Is something burning?"

Viv appeared in the doorway of our tiny kitchen, holding a wooden spoon. "God, I hate cooking."

"Give it to me." I grabbed the spoon as I walked past her. I peered into a pot of blackened rice.

"I don't think I added enough water," Viv said.

"Let's have eggs." I took the pot off the burner, nudged her out of the way and pulled a carton out of the fridge. My phone rang. I ignored it. Viv planted a sloppy kiss on my cheek. I could tell she'd been drinking. The smell of alcohol rose up like a cloud.

"I think there's some bread around here somewhere." Viv started rummaging in the cupboard.

"Try the breadbox," I said.

"Never thought of that," Viv mumbled.

We sat down to one of our dumpster specials—a dented can of baked beans, scrambled eggs and toast that was full of holes because we'd had to cut out the moldy bits. Viv kept forking up her eggs and putting them back on her plate. I watched her with a sinking feeling. The signs that something was up were definitely here.

She sat back in her chair and lit a joint.

"Okay. Just tell me." I pushed my plate away. No one was going to eat tonight, that was clear.

She didn't waste any time. She reached across the table and grabbed my hand. "Remember Javier from the bar? His band played there for two weeks just after Christmas. Name of the band is Rio Rock. Rock music with Latin influences.

Well, guess what?" She let go of my hand and spread her arms wide. "He asked me to go to South America with him."

"*South America?*"

"Yeah. Sandy beaches. Tropical breezes. Music all night long. Sexy Latin men who play guitars. 'The Girl from Ipanema'?"

"I know about South America, Viv. Although your cultural references are somewhat out of date."

"That's my brainy girl. Such a big vocabulary. *Cultural references*. Cool."

"So when do you leave?" I asked, ignoring her backhanded compliment.

"Tomorrow."

"*Tomorrow?*" I stood up and glared down at her. "That's pretty short notice. Even for you."

"I know, sweetie. But Javier is leaving tomorrow, and I want to go with him. No fun waiting till next month and having to travel alone."

"Not to mention that he could change his mind by then."

Viv's eyes teared up. "You could try being happy for me."

"What about me?"

"Stella. My star." Viv wiped her eyes. "You're young. You've got your whole life to live. Let me live mine."

As if she hadn't been living her life since forever. She'd been following bands around as long as I could remember. When I was little, she'd dragged me with her. When I got to be school age, she'd parked me with whoever would take me. But for the past five years, she would just up and leave me whenever she felt like it. I was left to deal by myself. I wanted to hate her. She put everything else before me. Always had. But looking at her sitting there so hopefully, waiting for me to give her permission, was hard. Like I was the parent and she was the kid.

I knew there was no use fighting it. She was going, and that was that. And who knew, maybe this guy would work out.

Somehow I highly doubted it.

"Yeah, go. Have fun. I'll take care of myself." I stacked the plates and scraped the eggs into the garbage.

Viv threw her arms around me and pecked me on the cheek. I got a whiff of patchouli as well as weed and whiskey.

"You could ask Felix," she said.

"My loser father isn't coming anywhere near me." I thought of the time he had come to see me in *The Little Mermaid* in fifth grade. He had roared into the school parking lot on his Harley with his latest girlfriend on the back. They had spent the whole play talking on their cell phones.

"Well, baby, life is a choice. You can choose to be happy or choose to be sad. I choose happy."

"Wow, Viv. That's very profound."

"I know, right?" She headed for her bedroom. "Got to pack."

My phone rang again just as her door closed. "Yeah, Marnie, what's up?"

"You are not going to believe it." Marnie's voice was a squeak. She was that excited.

"Believe what?"

"Turn on your TV. Channel 6. They're interviewing the lead singer of Razor. They've seen the cover you did of their song. The video now has eight thousand hits, by the way. They want to meet you."

Chapter Two

There he was. Wilcox MacKenzie, the lead singer of the best band ever. And he was talking about me.

"This kid has game. I like the way she slowed it down. Made it her own."

The hosts, a woman and a man, took turns interviewing Wilcox. "Tell us more about your tour dates," said the woman.

Wilcox rattled off ten cities, but the only one I cared about was Victoria. I so totally knew about that show, as I had desperately wanted to get tickets.

The male interviewer said, "The kid who posted that video lives in Victoria."

"Ooooh," said the woman. "Maybe you should try to meet her."

Wilcox looked uncomfortable. The guitar player sat forward. Ronnie Segal had the dangerous-bad-guy thing going on. Neck tats, a bald head covered in ink, an ink sleeve on both arms. "That's a great idea," said Ronnie with a side-long glance at Wilcox.

The interviewers were suddenly animated.

"Why don't we see if we can reach out to her?" asked the woman.

"Yes, I want to say right now that we are very interested in talking to her about joining us onstage. Have her sing a tune with the guys." Ronnie leaned back and smiled. Wilcox stared him down.

"Oh. My. God," Marnie said in my ear. I'd forgotten that I still had her on the phone. "Did you hear that?"

"No way I'm going to do this."

"*What*? Why not? This is the kind of break other people would kill for. You can thank me later." I heard computer keys clicking in the background. "Whoa. I already got a message from the TV station."

"I have to think," I said. The idea was terrifying. What if I sucked?

"I don't get it," Marnie said. "What's there to think about?"

"I'm not that good."

"Oh, come on! You got to work on that confidence, girl!"

The phone still stuck to my ear, I walked past Viv's closed door and into my room. The walls were plastered with posters of Razor. I loved their music.

I loved their sound. I had loved them since I was thirteen. But I'd never been able to afford tickets to see them live.

Viv opened her door and pushed her duffel bag into the hall. The smell of weed floated out too. Who knew when she'd be back. She was going to be somewhere in South America drinking margaritas, walking on the beach and perfecting her tan. Me? I was going to be busking in the freezing rain, dumpster diving for food and stuck here taking care of everything. Just like always.

"You know what?" I said to Marnie. "You're right. What have I got to lose? Give them my number."

"I already have a reply ready. All I have to do is hit *Send*…and done!"

We sat there for a few moments, Marnie on her end, me on mine. "Holy crap," Marnie said. "It's happening."

"Yeah. I doubt anything will come of it. They won't even read it. Bet it goes directly to spam."

"I love your positive thinking."

Viv poked her head into my room. She doesn't look anything like your typical mom. She is only sixteen years older than me. She just turned thirty-two, and there are lots of birthday cards on the table joking that she is over the hill, but she could easily pass for my sister. "Javier just called," she said, the multiple bracelets she wore on each arm jangling. "He wants to leave tonight."

"But Viv…"

She moved into the hall and beckoned for me to follow her out. "You have my cell-phone number. I don't know what the reception's like in South America, but you can always reach me through WhatsApp."

I wanted to tell her about the video. I thought she would be happy for me.

But then she put both hands on either side of my face. "Listen, Stell, I don't want anything to spoil this, okay? You have no idea what it has been like. I was changing diapers at your age. So what I want from you is for you to say, 'Have fun, Viv.' Repeat after me. Have fun, Viv." She gave me the best *I've sacrificed my whole life for you* look I'd seen yet.

I removed her hands from my face. Her pupils were huge. She ran her fingers through her wild hair. Waited. Looked me over.

"Have fun, Viv," I finally said.

She smiled. "That's my girl. Oh, there's tip money in the coffee tin to cover this month's rent. Call your father if you need more. It's about time he did something." She pointed at her duffel. "Carry that outside for me, okay?" She shouldered her backpack and started for the door.

We stood in the grungy doorway for maybe five minutes before Javier pulled up. A powdery snow, unusual for Victoria, had started to fall. Viv flung herself down the steps and into Javier's arms. I followed with her duffel. I looked away while Viv and Javier acted like they hadn't seen each other for months. Finally Javier took the duffel out of my outstretched hand and tossed it onto the back seat. Viv was already in the car. She poked her head out the window. "Remember to water the plant and feed the cat."

I blinked snow out of my eyes. "We don't have a cat."

"Give me a kiss, baby girl." She tapped her cheek.

I leaned over and kissed her. Javier honked as they drove around the corner. As their taillights faded, my phone dinged. I looked down. I had a text message from an unknown number.

We'd like to talk to you about appearing with the band Razor as a promotion for Rock 109. Can you get back to us? Loved your video!

Snow hit the screen and melted. I typed in a message.

Sure. Call me.

Then I went inside to throw up.

Chapter Three

I woke up at six o'clock the next morning with one thought in my head: What have I done? I called Marnie, who didn't sound too happy at being woken before the sun was up.

"Chill, would you?" Marnie yawned into the phone. "Just tell them you've changed your mind. Although I think you'd be stupid to do that."

"Maybe they won't even call."

"Whatever you say. I'm going back to sleep. Don't call again, okay?"

It was pitch black outside. The powdered-sugar snow was hanging on. It wasn't like I wasn't used to being alone. Viv had been leaving me on my own since I was twelve. I sat in the chair by the window and watched the streetlights go out. Then I showered and pulled on yesterday's jeans. I spiked my hair and lined my eyes in black. Loaded on the chains and stuffed my feet into my boots. There was no point hanging around the empty apartment.

I took the coffee tin out of the cupboard and popped the lid. I blinked in disbelief. She couldn't have. I shook the can, even though I knew there wasn't any point. Viv had lied. That was why she'd mentioned my father, something she'd never done before. There wasn't more than twenty dollars in loose change in the tin. She'd left me flat broke, and rent was due in two weeks. Despair clutched at my throat.

I stared at the tin for a full ten minutes, thinking I was imagining things. That there really was money in there and I just couldn't see it. Finally I stuffed all the change into my pocket. *What the hell?* I asked the empty, dirty apartment, *what the actual hell?* I decided I would go out for breakfast. A real breakfast. In a restaurant. Not at the dumpster behind it.

The coffee shop on the corner was just opening up. I was stupidly happy to see the lights. At least there was someone other than me out this early.

"Cold, eh?" A guy with a goatee flicked on switches. Machines hummed. Coffee dripped into big metal jugs. "You're up early. Coffee won't be ready for about ten minutes."

"No problem." I grabbed a seat by

the door. Mentally flipped through my busking playlist. I would have to do some serious time down at the waterfront over the next couple of weeks if I wanted to come even close to having enough money for rent. I thought about that stupid video and cringed.

The guy with the goatee had a name tag that said *Seth*. He brought me a coffee.

"Here," he said. "On the house. Because you're the first one here and you look like you really need it."

"Thanks." I wondered what he meant by that. Did I have *caffeine junkie* written on my forehead? Did I have giant bags under my eyes? What?

"Saw the video," said Seth a few minutes later when he brought me my food.

I didn't need to ask which video. My first instinct was to bolt for the door. Jeeez. My eyelid started to twitch.

"You're really good."

"Uh. Thanks." I tried to change the subject. "This coffee is delicious."

"It's the house blend. I roast the beans myself."

"Cool."

"So I hear you're going to sing with Razor. That true?"

"How do you know all this?" Now I was getting creeped out.

"I'm Marnie's cousin. And FB friend. She forwarded the YouTube link to everyone she's ever met. She could seriously be a promoter."

"You're right about that," I said.

"So are you going to do it? Sing with them?"

"Yeah. I guess so." It had just occurred to me that maybe they would pay me. Probably not much, but I was desperate.

"Cool. I've got tickets for the show. That's going to be something."

"I'm not so sure." My heart was racing, and I was pretty sure the caffeine had nothing to do with it. The concert was only a day away.

"You'll be great. Anyway, got to get back to work." Just as he said that, three people blew in, trying to get out of the rain that was splattering the window. I wolfed down my breakfast, bundled up and left enough change on the table to cover my meal. I was glad Seth had put my coffee in a to-go cup. As I opened the door to leave, he yelled after me, "Good luck! You'll kill it!"

I forced myself to smile and wave. The only thing I wanted to kill was Marnie. I had stopped to take a sip of my coffee when my phone dinged. I pulled it out. There was a string of messages I'd missed while I was eating. The local TV station wanted me to come in after school to do an interview. Razor's manager wanted to talk to me about a rehearsal. Releases needed to be signed. And there was one from an unknown number. It just said, **Call me. Wilcox.**

I practically spit my coffee out. I was getting text messages from Razor's lead singer? I hit Marnie's number.

"Yeah?" She sounded wider awake than she had earlier, but not by much.

"Wilcox MacKenzie wants to talk to me."

"Seriously?"

"What am I going to do?"

"Call him. Stop being such a wuss. You've got this."

I went to the park next to the big cathedral. It was cold this morning, but there were a couple of humans slumped on benches. There had been an entire community of homeless people living in the park until the city had forced them to move. My mind was jumping all over the place. Wilcox MacKenzie wanted me to call him. I finished off my coffee and watched the ragged bundles come to life. I still had an hour until school started. I decided to take a walk.

I headed to Beacon Hill Park. Seeing the animals in the petting zoo brought up some of my best childhood memories. Viv had brought me here on weekends she was around because it was free and she didn't know what else to do. We'd hang out, watch the goats. Goats will get you every time. They are stupidly funny.

The petting zoo wasn't working its magic this morning though. All I could think about was that I was expected to sing with a band the whole world knew. I desperately wanted to ask Viv for advice. She wasn't much of a parent, and I was really pissed off at her, but she was my mother, and if she knew anything at all, it was how bands work.

My phone chased away that dumb idea. Probably Marnie, I thought as I

fished it out of my jacket pocket. But no.
It was Wilcox. It was the same number
he'd texted me from. The number had
seared itself onto my brain. I stared at
the phone as it kept ringing. Holy crap,
I thought. Holeee crap.

Then I brought the phone to my ear
and answered it. "Hello?"

Chapter Four

The manager met me at the entrance to the arena. "Hey, I'm Gordon," he said, shaking my hand. "You must be Stella. Come backstage and meet the guys." His long gray ponytail was thin at the ends. I couldn't help but notice, as he led me down the aisle and up onto the stage, that his belly hung over the belt on his too-tight jeans. Each step of the way, my heart thudded. Roadies carried equipment, dragged cables, tested lights. My head kept sending me urgent alerts that the show was on *Friday*.

The dressing-room door just said *Wilcox*. No last name. The manager knocked loudly. "Hey, it's Gordon. I've got the kid with me."

Kid? I might be sixteen, but I was no kid. I wanted to point this out, but just then the door opened and Wilcox MacKenzie was looking me up and down.

"So you're the voice. Come on in." There were instruments leaning against or on top of every chair. Wilcox moved an acoustic guitar off the couch beside him and pointed. "Here. Come sit."

Gordon leaned against the bar fridge in the corner. Wilcox shifted him aside, opened the fridge and grabbed a can of beer. He handed it to me, and I wondered if it was some kind of test.

"Thanks," I said.

He cracked the tab on a second beer and took a big swig. I did the same.

"So," he said, sitting down beside me. "You're going to do a number with us, hey?" I nodded. The beer was already going to my head. I put the can on the floor. "You're sixteen?" Wilcox took another long drink.

"I'll be seventeen next month."

"So your parents are cool with this?" Gordon asked.

"Yeah." If they knew Viv, I thought, they wouldn't even ask.

"Do we need to get their permission?"

"No. She's sixteen," said Gordon. "It's fine for her do this without asking anyone."

"All right then." Wilcox looked me in the eyes. "We all liked that video." He smiled the smile that made female fans turn to jelly. "So what gave you the idea to slow the song down like that?"

"It always felt like a ballad to me."

"Why?"

"It talks about losing things you love. Razor's version is angry. But I always thought the words were sad."

Wilcox watched me over his beer can as he took another swig. His eyes were charcoal colored. His hair was black. His tattoos were indigo. "I want you to do it slow on Friday, just like in the video. That was a cappella, but I'm going to play with you. So we're going to have to rehearse." He picked up his guitar and strummed it. The chords of "Long Gone" filled the dressing room. "I thought we'd pare it all down. Make it a moment. We call you out to a single spotlight and a standing mic. I accompany you with the acoustic, and you sing. No frills. What do you think?"

What did I think? I thought, Where can I run for safety? I thought, I can't believe Wilcox MacKenzie is asking for my opinion. I thought, I need another drink. I picked up the beer. Wilcox studied me. Gordon stepped outside to answer a phone call. "Sure," I said. "That sounds good."

"Come with me." Wilcox stood and headed for the door. Gordon nodded as we passed him, his phone still glued to his ear. Next thing I knew we were on the stage. Wilcox pulled a three-legged stool to the center of the stage. "I'll sit here." He pointed at a mark on the floor three feet away. "The mic will be there." He yelled to someone manning a bank of electronic equipment. "Jones. Give us a single! Ferney, bring up a mic."

A sudden flash made my eyes water. I was standing in a cone of light. Dust floated in the air, and a small, wiry guy appeared with a mic, which he adjusted to my height. Wilcox sat on the stool, strummed the guitar he'd brought with him from the dressing room and nodded at me. "Let's see how it sounds."

The activity in the room stopped. Everyone stared at me. My legs were in real danger of crumpling like tissue paper.

Wilcox hit the opening chords. "At the count of four," he said quietly.

I closed my eyes. The lyrics appeared in the blackness of my mind. To calm myself, I thought of space. I imagined stars and the planets floating above me. I thought how they stretched out forever and ever and ever. I thought how we were nothing more than tiny specks. Unimportant, tiny specks. Then, just to be on the safe side, I imagined that everyone staring at me was naked.

I started to sing, slowing the familiar tune way down like I had in the video. I liked the sound of the guitar behind me. I liked the way my voice echoed as it hit the rafters.

Phantoms in the air
Crashing all around me
Telling me that life won't last
Everything will come and go
Like pain, like love, like what you said

Long gone
Long gone
Baby you are long gone
Take your pain and take your love
Give me back my sanity

Phantoms everywhere
Like happiness and trust and joy
The way you looked, the plans we made
Long gone

Long gone
Long gone
Baby you are long gone
Take your pain and take your lies
And give me back my sanity

The last note faded. I opened my eyes. No one spoke.

"Hell," someone said from the back of the room. "That was a downer. But in a good way."

Chapter Five

Wilcox motioned for me to follow him to the dressing room. "That was great. But I want to work on a couple of places," he said after we'd settled back on the couch. "See how the chorus picks up on this chord?" He strummed a G minor.

"Yeah."

"I want you to hold the note a beat longer. Feel the pain. Make it real."

He sang the words *long gone* and somehow made them sound devastating.

"That was beautiful." I really meant it. It was easy to see why he was a star.

"I've never thought of the song this way, as sad, like you said. I wrote it about someone who left me, and I was angry, so angry. I wanted to use the song to rake that person over the coals. To say all the things I never got to say to their face. But I can see how that *is* sad. Even pathetic." He smiled. My heart thudded.

"I always wondered who that song was about."

"I like to keep people guessing," he said. "But I really want to know what *you* are thinking when you sing it."

I was thinking of Viv, but I didn't want to tell him that. How lame to take an angry breakup song and make it about how your mother never loved you, how she'd take off without a backward look if there was a guy to follow around. "Just a guy."

"You're pretty young to have such a broken heart."

"Yeah, well. Heartbreak can happen to anyone."

Wilcox leaned back and crossed his legs. I tried not to stare at his tattoos. Or the way they kind of rippled when he strummed his guitar. Or the way his charcoal eyes were assessing me.

The door to his dressing room swung open. Ronnie leaned against the door frame, his arms crossed over his chest. His mouth was a thin line. Some kind of dark energy was coming off him. He looked totally pissed off. I jumped to my feet. Wilcox shot Ronnie an intense look.

Ronnie pushed off from the door frame. "I need to talk to you, Wilcox," he said. "Now," He turned and headed down the hallway.

Wilcox kept strumming his guitar, talking to me like nothing weird had just happened. It was like he was trying to drag things out as long as possible. He closed his eyes and kind of zoned out, singing the chorus in a soft and sad voice, just like I had. "I may cut a new version of this song," he said. "Maybe even get you to sing a duet with me. How would you feel about that?"

"Are you kidding? That would be unbelievable."

He smiled in a way that rocked my world. My breath caught in my throat. I couldn't speak.

"So let's meet here tomorrow at six. Rehearse the song a couple more times before you go on. You cool with that?"

"Sure." I felt anything but cool. My pits felt like sinkholes.

"Great." He studied me. "Talk to Gordon on the way out. He's got some paperwork for you." His phone rang.

He glanced at the caller ID and nodded at me. "I have to take this. Close the door on your way out."

Gordon caught up with me in the hall. "Here, sign this." He shoved a paper at me. "It's a release form." He led me into a room with a couch and a dressing table.

At the table I scribbled my name on the dotted line. Gordon nodded. "So you got your instructions?" he asked. "Be here tomorrow at six? The show's at eight. You'll go on right before intermission. And the TV station wants to interview you when you come offstage. Here's what I want you to say. The band saw your video and wanted to give you a shot. The media loves that angle. They will play up how they brought the video to Razor's attention. So be ready to kill it tomorrow. No pressure. Heh."

No pressure, right. I left the arena feeling a bit sick.

Marnie was waiting outside. She looked mad. "I tried to tell those bozos that I am friends with their new star, but they wouldn't believe me. Or let me in." She scowled at the security guards standing near the main doors. "I thought about making a run for it, but they look like they could literally squash me. Why aren't you answering my texts?" Her hair was sticking out from under her watch cap. "It's freaking cold out here."

She finally stopped rambling "I turned my phone off," I replied. "We were rehearsing."

"So? How did it go?" Marnie hooked her arm through mine. "Let's get coffee. Did I say it's freezing out here?"

The coffee shop was busy. Lots of steamy drinks were being made as people tried to fight the cold and the dark.

"Tell me everything," Marnie said. "What's he like?"

"I assume you mean Wilcox."

"No, the big, ugly bouncer at the front door." Marnie cocked her eyebrow. "*Yes*, Wilcox."

"He's pretty chill. We rehearsed. He's tall." I left out how he always touched my arm when he wanted to get my attention. Or how he pressed my diaphragm to show me how to breathe. Or how his smile left burn marks on my eyeballs. Or how he'd actually said he'd like to do a duet with me.

"Tall? Who cares if he's tall?"

"I don't really know what else to tell you. It's not like he was raving drunk or anything. He was focused on the gig."

"He's got a reputation. Trashed that hotel room in Seattle."

"Yeah, well. He seemed low-key to me." I hoped I was pulling it off. The indifference. In reality, my heart was still pounding from the thrill of our session and the idea that I could sing with him. Marnie sipped her coffee. Maybe she was buying it. Her phone had dinged twenty times in the fifteen minutes we'd been sitting here. It must be killing her not to read her texts. "Go ahead." I nodded at her phone.

"You don't mind? I've been telling everyone I know about this. They are all trying to get tickets. Hey, do you think you could help with that?"

"How?"

"Bands always set aside tickets for personal use. Maybe you could ask Wilcox for, like, ten?"

"*Ten*?"

"Six?"

"I don't know."

"Come on. You got to get something out of the deal. Plus you owe me. Big-time." Marnie flashed her best best-friend smile, but I knew she was serious. She expected some payback.

"Yeah, maybe," I said.

Marnie tapped my phone. "Text him. Now. I want to let your fan club know if they're going to see you in action. Concert's tomorrow."

"I suppose it wouldn't hurt." Truth was, I hated asking anyone for anything. My finger hovered over my phone. I typed the ask, closed my eyes and hit *Send*.

"Good girl," Marnie said. She swung around in her seat. "Hey, Jared!" A guy from school was standing outside. He saw Marnie wave and came in and sat down with us. "It's on. We're just waiting to hear," she said.

"Cool."

"What's going on?" I asked. I didn't know Jared except to see him in the hall. He had a skeezy reputation.

"If you score some freebies, Jared here is your man. He can scalp those babies. We can split the cash three ways. Six tickets to this sold-out concert?

Big bucks. Probably a couple hundred for each of us."

"No."

"What? You couldn't use some extra money? With Viv gone again?"

"How did you know she was gone?"

"She told my mom she was bailing. Like she always does whenever she gets hot and heavy with her latest music man. Only this guy is the real deal, according to what she told my mom. She may not be back this time." Marnie reached over and rubbed my arm. "I'm doing this for you. You got bills to pay."

She may not be back this time. I shoved that thought to the back of my mind. I couldn't think about Viv when I had so much going on. This scalping thing, for example. I didn't like it. But Marnie and I had been friends since kindergarten. I'd spent lots of weekends at her place when Viv was MIA. We'd gone through the My Little Pony phase together. Then the Ariel-the-mermaid phase. But in the past year Marnie had started hanging out with kids who did stuff I didn't think was cool. Shoplifting. Smoking weed. Skipping school. But she was still my best friend. And she had a point. I did have bills to pay. Maybe just this one time…

"It's not like you're the first person ever to ask for free tickets." Marnie dumped another packet of sugar into her coffee.

"I've got lots of rich kids lined up to score tickets to this concert," Jared said. "All I need are the goods."

"And Stella here is going to deliver." Marnie slapped a lid on her cup. "I have to go. Dinner with the fam. Got to keep the parents happy. Know what I mean?"

Jared stood up too. "I have places to be too, kids. Later."

They fist-bumped each other and headed for the door.

I sat there. Alone. Wishing Marnie had asked me for dinner. I wondered if she and Jared were an item. If so, when had that happened? Tears pressed at the back of my eyes. There was an ache inside my chest where my heart was supposed to be. I wanted to talk to Viv. True, she wasn't much of a parent, but she was all I had.

Felix, the drummer in a dead-end band, had been a one-night stand. He'd never been present in my life. He had never wanted to be a father in the first place, Viv told me. She had raised me on her own, and for the first four years of my life we'd never stayed in one place for more than a few months. She was always following a guy. The guy who had landed us in Victoria had lasted eighteen months, longer than most. But Victoria had suited us, so we stayed.

Viv had started working at bars around town, although she still took off occasionally when some musician caught her eye. I'd started school. Got jobs as soon as I could to help her out. As for my father? He'd taken off to Vancouver, and other than the one time he came to see my play, I never saw him. Viv said he'd gotten married and now had two more kids. It was like I didn't exist. Not that I was complaining. Who needs a cruddy father like that?

I pitched my empty cup in the trash and pulled my hat low onto my forehead. I had to find something to eat. With less than five dollars in my pocket, dumpster diving was my best option. Viv and I did it all the time. "The things people throw out," she'd say as she hauled a barely expired wheel of Brie cheese out of a bin behind some expensive grocery store. I wasn't in the mood to forage, but I didn't like using the food bank. The cans were dented, and the crap was really old, mostly made up of stuff no one ever used. Mmm, kidney beans. Plus the place was crawling with do-gooders. Some of them were parents of the kids I went to school with. I did not need the added drama of that.

Maybe scoring a few bucks on some concert tickets wasn't such a bad thing. My phone pinged. A text from Wilcox.

Sure. I can give you six tickets. I'll leave them at the box office for you. Wilcox.

I texted back my thanks.

This would make Marnie so happy. Why then, I wondered as a hot tear plopped onto the screen, was I suddenly reluctant to give her the news?

Chapter Six

All I did from the time I went to bed until the time I got up was stare at the wall and try to convince myself I wasn't going to heave. How had I gotten myself into this? What if I blanked on the lyrics? My throat was raw. Was I getting strep? I wanted to talk to Wilcox. His hand on my arm was soothing and exciting at the same time. He would know how to calm me down.

When I wasn't thinking about the way Wilcox had looked at me, or stressing about the show, I was freaking out about money. With what I had in the bank, plus whatever I might get from the ticket sales, I figured I was okay for a month or two. But what about after that? I could make maybe a couple hundred bucks busking down at the waterfront. It was February, after all, and tourists were in short supply. What kind of mother takes off and leaves her kid busted? A groupie pothead, said a nasty voice inside me.

I had exactly two pairs of black jeans, and both needed washing. I chose the cleanest ones from the pile on the floor and found a T-shirt of Viv's that said *Everybody Lies*. How appropriate, I thought. It was from her done-with-men phase. Which lasted all of ten minutes. At least the T-shirt was black, so it worked just fine.

I like lists, so I made one. *Go to school. Go to the box office after school and get the tickets. Give the tickets to Marnie. Meet Wilcox to rehearse. Die of fear.*

Oh, and somewhere along the line I was going to have to find a dumpster without a security camera so I could score some more food. I moved dumpster diving to the top of my list. I needed to eat or I might faint. I sent the universe an order for blueberry muffins. Not more than one day old. There was a decent dumpster on Fort Street near Foul Bay Road. I'd check it out on my way to school. A plan always gave me a sense of control. I gargled with some salt water, poured what was left of my coffee into a travel mug and went in search of breakfast.

Chapter Seven

I sat on the park bench and washed down the last of the desert-dry pumpkin scone I'd scored to have with my lukewarm coffee. Scones weren't my favorite, but that was all the universe had seen fit to deliver. It was too cold outside to sit for long. I headed for the box office on the way to school, hoping it was open. Nope. Sign said it would open at noon.

I was just leaving when a long black limo pulled up.

When it got closer, the back window rolled down.

It was Gordon. Not the ride I'd expected for the manager of a rock band.

"Hi, Stella!" He waved me over. "You're here early."

"So are you."

"Tell me about it." He rummaged around on the seat and grabbed an envelope. "Wilcox wanted you to have these. I was just about to drop them at the box office. But here you are. You got family coming?"

"Friends." I nodded.

"Where are your parents? I never did ask you that."

"My mother's in South America right now." I tried to make it sound like this was normal. Like she traveled all the time. Like for an important job or something. "My dad's in Vancouver. He can't get here on such short notice."

Gordon looked at me like he wasn't buying it. "No brothers or sisters?"

"Nope. Only child."

He handed me the envelope through the window. "Well, I hope your friends enjoy the show." I reached for the envelope, and he held it just a beat too long before he let it go.

"Thanks. I know they will."

The limo rolled past me and turned into the arena's underground parking.

The tickets burned a hole in my pocket all the way to school. Scalping these tickets wasn't illegal. But it still didn't feel good. It felt skeezy.

I spotted Jared and Marnie hanging around by the smokers. Marnie waved me over. I thought about pretending I hadn't seen her. But she knew me too well. I could never fake her out. "Your face is a dead giveaway," she told me every time I tried to. "You're not that good an actress."

"Jared has already sold every ticket," Marnie said, meeting me halfway and kissing my cheek in greeting. For some reason that reminded me of the Saturday sleepovers when her mom gave us heart- and star-shaped Rice Krispie treats and chocolate milkshakes for breakfast. "When are you going to get them?"

I handed her the envelope like a flag of surrender. "It just so happens I ran into Razor's manager on my way to school."

Marnie squealed. "Hey, Jared! Get over here!" She waved the envelope.

Jared sauntered over. "Good deal, Stell." He opened the envelope and counted the tickets. "I'll take a run out to St. Francis this afternoon and pick up the cash." St. Francis was the private school the rich kids went to.

Drove to, I should say. In their BMWs. Jared stuffed the envelope in his backpack and went back to the smokers.

Marnie hooked her arm through mine. "How are you holding up?"

"It's scary," I said, my voice shaking. "I'm freaking out a bit."

"You'll be great. You're always great." She squeezed my arm.

I squeezed her back. It felt like old times. Like when we were ten and both of us cut off our ponytails to donate to Locks of Love and got our pictures in the local paper. Or when we were twelve and got our periods within months of each other. Or even the previous year when, for our birthdays, so we'd never forget those sleepovers, she got a heart and I got a star tattooed on the inside of our wrists. I took a deep breath and told myself everything was going to be okay. That I would get through this day, get through the song and somehow manage to survive until Viv decided to come back.

Max, a guy in our grade, saw us heading toward the school and held the door open for us. "Saw your video," he said as Marnie and I passed him. "You nailed that tune. Could I talk to you for a minute?"

Marnie was already a few steps ahead of me. "Hey, Jared, wait up!" she yelled. She looked back at me. "See you in a bit, Stell."

Max is one of the guys who just shows up, gets his work done and leaves. It's like he's just putting in his time until graduation so he can get on with his real life. He's in a band that actually gets paying gigs. Truth is, I've been crushing on him for a year. He's six feet tall, slicks his brown hair back and has really good teeth. Which makes his smile killer. He was flashing it at me as he spoke.

"What's up?" I asked.

"You know I play in a band, Pod?" I nodded. "Well, we do a lot of gigs around town and up-island. Last summer we even toured for a month on the mainland. I'd love for you to come out and meet us. We could use your talents." Again the killer smile.

"I guess I could come to one of your sessions." I tried to sound low-key even though my heart was jumping rope. Max's band had serious street cred. Their latest single had even got radio play.

"I know you're singing with Razor tonight. Word's out all over social media. I've got tickets, so I'll get to see you live."

My phone dinged at the same time as the final bell rang. "Cool," I said, even though knowing he would be at the show only made me more nervous. "Sorry, I've got to get this." He nodded but didn't move. I guess he didn't care if he was late for class.

The text was from the radio station. They wanted me to come in for an interview at noon. Then I got a text from Gordon. He was checking to make sure I was still planning to get to the theater at six.

Max watched me. "It's happening," he said, nodding at the string of texts lighting up my screen. "You want some advice? Probably not, but here it is anyway. Take this thing on your terms. Everyone is going to want a piece of you. Try to stay whole."

"Was that the sound of bubbles bursting?" I tried for a joke, but judging by the look on Max's face, it had landed badly.

"Maybe." Max rubbed the back of his neck. "Something like this happened to me when I was fourteen. They wanted to turn me into the next Justin Bieber.

I almost went for it until I realized it wasn't my scene. If you ever want to talk to someone who gets it, give me a call. In the meantime, I'll let the guys know you're up for jamming with us. How about Sunday?"

"Sure. Sunday should work."

He reached for my phone. I handed it to him before I even realized what I was doing.

"Great. Good luck tonight." He entered his contact details into my phone. "I'll text you the address." He touched my shoulder. Then he headed down the corridor toward the science labs.

My arm tingled, but my feet were frozen. My face burned and my stomach heaved.

How had my life gone from boring to this in just two days?

Chapter Eight

Backstage was a blur of moving parts.
The interview with the radio station had
gone well, but it had jangled my nerves.
Now everywhere I looked, people were
running around as if they had the most
important job in the world. I tried some
deep breathing—in and out, in and out.
Didn't do much good.

Gordon spotted me from the door of Wilcox's dressing room. "Stella, there you are. Wilcox wants to see you."

Yes, that's why I'm here, dude, I thought. Gordon seemed to be wired pretty tight.

Wilcox was sitting on the couch, long legs extended and crossed at the ankles. He strummed his guitar, that faraway look on his face. "Come. Sit," he said. He nodded at Gordon. "Thanks, man."

I perched on the edge of the couch. Wilcox played for a few more minutes in silence. Finally he spoke. "Good interview."

"Oh! Thanks. I'm surprised you had time to listen."

"Gordon recorded it. You sounded nervous. Which is endearing. Puts people on your side. Like an underdog."

I didn't know what to say to that. I swallowed.

"All right then. Let's run through this a few times." He took my hand. He held it all the way to the stage. My palm was so greasy from nerves, it probably felt to him like he was holding a stick of butter. "Okay, remember your mark?" He pointed at the tape on the floor. I nodded. "Try to stay as close to that spot as you can for the whole song. Okay, from the top."

The first run-through was a bit bumpy. We ended up doing it three more times. Each time felt better. By the end of the fourth, I knew it was going to be okay. Wilcox leaned his guitar against the stool and stood up. "Cool. I'll see you later."

I could have sworn he had been about to say something else. But then he was gone. I wondered if he even remembered talking about doing a duet together.

Gordon appeared from the wings. "Kid, that was great! You should think about getting an agent." He slapped me on the back. "I can recommend a few people."

A woman wearing an apron with pockets stuffed full of cosmetics called my name. "Let's get you into hair and makeup." She motioned for me to follow her. "My name's Samantha," she told me as she caked my face with foundation, outlined my eyes in black and spiked my hair. "You've got a great look. We just need to emphasize it for this size of venue." The lighted mirror made me look like a ghost with black eyes.

There was a long table loaded with trays of fruit, cheese and bagels. I hadn't eaten anything since the dry, day-old pumpkin scone that morning. I was starving, but my stomach was too knotted to eat. I tried more deep breathing, but all it did was make me cough. It was only an hour until showtime. I could tell by the change in sound that the doors had opened. People were piling in, and a weird kind of electricity filled the air. I peeked out at the audience from behind the stage curtain. The reserved seats in the front rows were filled with kids I'd seen around town. Jared was there, and I wondered if he'd kept one of the comp tickets for himself. I saw Max and three other guys make their way down the aisle. He was easy to spot because of his height.

The room buzzed as people greeted each other. The energy was building and ran through me like a current. I let the curtain fall. It was better not to obsess about who was out there. I wished Marnie was with me. Or Viv.

The band members of Razor swept by on their way to the stage. None of them said a word to me. They were in the zone. The concert was about to start. Gordon took my elbow and steered me to the spot where I was supposed to wait until it was time for my entrance. Spotlights crisscrossed the room.

Wilcox stepped up to the standing microphone at the front of the stage and yelled, "Hello, Victoria!" The drummer hit the crash cymbals, and Ronnie squealed out the familiar opening chords of "Gotcha Coming." The crowd started screaming. The special effects kicked in, and smoke began to rise from the stage. The concert was off and running.

The set started loud and noisy and built from there. Sweat poured off Wilcox's face. My eyes were glued to his every move. And then. The sounds from the last song faded and the room quieted. Stagehands pulled the stool to center stage. The blaring lights faded. The rest of the band walked offstage. Wilcox stood alone in a cone of light.

"We've got something really special for you tonight. Some of you might have seen this talented artist on YouTube.

When I saw her perform, I couldn't resist inviting her up here to sing with me." The crowd whistled and hooted. "Yeah, never mind." Wilcox laughed. "Let's just say this talented lady is going places. Her name means 'star,' after all. And mark my words, she's going to be one. Let's hear it for Stella Connors!"

The crowd howled.

Gordon whispered in my ear. "You're on." He nudged me.

Wilcox looked offstage at me and held out his hand.

And with legs like a newborn deer's, I walked out into the spotlight.

Chapter Nine

It was as if someone had blasted the entire room with a stun gun. Everyone went quiet. Could they hear my breathing? A thousand pairs of eyes watched my every echoing step. I told myself to focus on putting one foot in front of the other. The mic was my lifeline. Wilcox was on the stool, his guitar resting on one knee, his boot heel hooked over the bottom rung. He nodded as I got closer. It was impossible to rip my eyes off the floor. Then I heard a soft "One, two, three, four," and the opening chords of "Long Gone" rippled out into the arena. Slow, haunting, sad. Just like we'd rehearsed.

It was muscle memory more than anything else that got me started. My hands gripped the mic. The music seeped into my brain. My mouth opened. Thoughts of Viv took over. First came the memories of moving so often I couldn't remember the names of the towns we'd lived in. "*Long gone, long gone…*" Leaving my dog behind because we'd been evicted. "*The way you looked, the plans we made…*" The times she left me alone to follow her latest guy. "*Everything will come and go…*"

By the second chorus, the song had started to build. I finally looked up when I hit the high note on "*give me back my sanity*…" If notes were living things, that note would have beaten against the spotlight like a moth. It danced in the air, folded its wings and died away.

I saw Max in the crowd. He was on his feet, cheering. Behind me, I heard Wilcox put down the guitar and stand up. The legs of the stool scratched on the wooden floor. Applause broke over me like a wave. I forced a smile. I sensed Wilcox stepping into the spotlight with me. "Take a bow," he whispered. "That was amazing."

I bowed my head. Faces jumped out at me. Jared, four-finger whistling. Gordon, in the wings, on the phone. Samantha, holding a curling iron, wiping a tear. Wilcox, with a look in his eyes I couldn't figure out.

"Stella Connors, everyone!" Wilcox shouted, and the crowd erupted again. He put his hand on my back and guided me off the stage.

Samantha embraced me. Gordon grabbed me and took me to his "office." A crew from the radio station was there, on remote, asking questions. "How did it feel? Do you know your life just changed? What do you have to say to Wilcox?"

I can't remember how I answered. But when they finally left, Gordon came over and sat beside me. "The band wants you to come with them to Vancouver next Friday. Then hook up with them next month. You got a break in March, right? Perform in a few more cities. Think about it. We can talk dollars later." He headed for the door, phone to his ear as usual.

I was alone. My stomach howled, reminding me I hadn't eaten all day. I stepped into the corridor. Roadies were setting up for the second half of the show. The band was nowhere to be seen. I don't know what I expected or if

I expected anything at all. But now that it was over, I wasn't sure what to do. Through a half-open door I saw Wilcox talking to one of the tall, gorgeous women who seemed to be everywhere. Samantha was powdering Ronnie's bald head. He scowled when he saw me. The radio crew was now interviewing members of the crowd. The moment had flatlined. I found my coat and headed for the stage door. Outside, I gulped the fresh, salty air.

I was so broke, I couldn't even buy coffee. I should have grabbed some food from the tables backstage. It didn't matter. The angry hunger beast had gone back to sleep. I didn't want to go to my empty apartment, so I walked toward Government Street. The lights of the Inner Harbour made me feel more alone, so I turned toward Beacon Hill Park. The petting zoo would be closed, but I could sit outside the fence and watch the animals sleep. I wondered what Wilcox was doing. Was he looking for me? Why hadn't I hung around to socialize with the band after the show? For some reason I thought of Viv. What bar in South America was she sitting in right now? I sighed.

Next week, I would have to go back to school. Get my cut of the ticket sales from Jared. Pay the rent. Buy some food. It was starting to drizzle, so I hitched up the hood on my sweatshirt and found a spot under an oak tree. A goat with a brown eye patch stared at me through the fence.

My phone lit up. A text from Wilcox.

Where are you? We're having a party. You should be here.

My heart leaped.

Then another text. This one from Marnie.

You killed it. You want to hang? We're at Jared's.

Then another. From Max.

Pure gold tonight. Don't forget our jam on Sunday.

The goat blinked at me. A shooting star soared over the ocean.

I inhaled the cold air, hardly daring to breathe. Wilcox wanted me. I put my phone in my pocket and headed back to the arena.

Chapter Ten

Pod was a great band. All original material. A new-age Nirvana. There were six other members, and no one really seemed to care that I'd sung with Razor on Friday night. Or that I'd be doing it again in Vancouver this coming Friday. Or that I could be touring with them in March.

It didn't matter. After the party I knew I couldn't wait to be with Wilcox again. The room had been filled with band members and crew. Drinks had flowed. Wilcox had sat me on his knee while Gordon took pictures. I'd taken a selfie of the two of us. He was kissing me on the cheek, his arm draped over my shoulder. I was thinking of posting it on Instagram. He'd talked about how I'd maybe get a permanent place in the band but seemed to have completely forgotten our duet. I didn't care. He kept saying I could go on tour with them. Not like a groupie, but as a part of the band. The idea had thrilled me. Then Viv had snuck into my head. *I'm going to be the manager, honey. Revere said I could do the bookings. How about that?* That deal hadn't lasted more than two weeks. Not the same, I'd told myself. So, so, so not the same.

"You ever write anything?" asked Pod's drummer, a guy named Vance.

I nodded shyly.

Max stopped tuning his guitar and said, "I'd love to take a listen."

My mind off-ramped from the dream of my road trip with Razor. My face could have been mistaken for a tomato, it was so red. Squash me now, I thought.

"When you're ready," he added, realizing how uncomfortable I was. "Today I'd love you to try this tune." He handed me a sheet of paper with some scrawled lyrics. "I wrote this a few months ago, but I really felt it needed a female voice. You want to give it a go?"

The rest of the band settled into their spots. They ran through a couple of the songs I'd heard them play around town while I read over Max's song. I was stunned by how it affected me. The words somehow dove straight into my heart.

"So what do you think of the lyrics?" Max asked me after a while. He was standing over me.

I swallowed the ball of feelings in my throat. "Really good."

Max smiled like he really cared what I thought. "I hoped you'd like it. Want to give it a try?"

The other guys were swigging drinks. Coffee. Beer. Water. They weren't paying much attention to us as they compared set notes and talked about minor adjustments. "Yeah." I stood up.

"Great." Max grabbed his guitar and took me out into the backyard. It was cold, but it wasn't raining. He handed me a mug of coffee and pointed to a picnic table. "Over there."

He strummed a few chords. "The melody starts like this." He sang in a low voice. The tune wafted in the air like a strand of milkweed on the wind.

That's what the song was called. "Milkweed." Max kept going until I wiped a tear away. "That bad, eh?"

"I love it."

Max smiled. "You try."

I closed my eyes and felt the music. Sang it the way he had. Soft and intimate, like a prayer.

"Wow." Max put down his guitar. "I was right about it needing a female voice. That was perfect."

We turned as two of the band members applauded. They'd come onto the patio without our noticing. "Nice," said Jim, the bass player. "You going to try it with the band now?"

By the time we finished for the day, the song was as much mine as it was theirs. They'd asked me to think about joining them permanently. A week earlier it would have been a dream come true. But today? Today it was a letdown after the high-voltage charge of hanging with Razor. Still, we'd connected so well. Like a real band. It was such a good feeling that I did something I never thought I'd do. As we headed down the walk, I pulled my notebook out of my backpack.

"What's this?" asked Max when I handed it to him.

"Some of my songs." I gulped. "Would you look at them and tell me what you think?" Despite the cold, a waterfall of perspiration was flowing down my spine.

Max took the notebook and turned it over. I had scrawled graffiti and doodles all over it. He ran his thumb over the cover slowly and gently. "I feel I've just been given an amazing gift."

That was exactly what I needed to hear. But I couldn't speak. I turned and ran. I didn't stop until I was around the corner and knew he could no longer see me.

Later that day, when I tried to explain my confusion to Marnie, she thought I'd lost my mind. "You've got to go with Razor!" she insisted.

I couldn't make her understand. Walking around in the dark. Talking to the goat. Partying with Wilcox. How performing with Razor and Wilcox had lit a fire inside me. A fire I didn't even know was there. But also how jamming with Pod had made me feel like a true musician.

Marnie was lounging on my bed. She rolled over onto her stomach. "Don't let a bunch of local yokels pull you down," she said, like the decision was hers. And easy. She draped herself over the edge of the bed and counted out my money on the floor. As I suspected, it was short because Jared had kept one of the tickets for himself. I didn't say anything. It was a lot more money than I'd had the day before. Still, I thought Jared should at least deduct his ticket price from his cut.

"Max asked me to jam with his group again, maybe even join Pod permanently."

Marnie cocked an eyebrow. "You going to?"

"Maybe."

"Don't give it away. Who knows, maybe Razor will want to add you permanently."

"I don't think so. To them I'm just a novelty. They'll get tired of it all soon." I didn't tell her how Gordon had asked me about doing a couple of shows over spring break.

"I'm not so sure about that. Anyway. Don't let Max suck you into his band. Now isn't the time to be closing doors, kiddo. Now that the world is watching you."

"Oh god, Marnie. Don't make this into *A Star Is Born*. It was one shot. Maybe two. Then they'll go away, and my fifteen minutes of fame will be over." I felt Wilcox's hand on my back. His breath on my hair while I sat on his lap. Mentally counted the minutes until the Vancouver show.

"Spoken like the true pessimist you are." Marnie got off the bed. "So have you heard from Viv?"

"Not since she left."

"It must be so cool not having a parent breathing down your neck all the time." Marnie bent and kissed my cheek. "Speaking of which, I've got to go. My evil mom is taking me shopping."

"Doesn't sound so evil to me."

"Wait till you see the preppie clothes she'll try to push on me."

After Marnie left, I scrolled through my messages and deleted them all except the one from Wilcox.

Leaving for Vancouver tonight. Come by the hotel this afternoon and we can talk before we go.

I texted back.

How about now?

I got a reply immediately.

Cool

When I got to the hotel, half the band members were eating in the restaurant. Wilcox was sitting in the lobby, reading *The Catcher in the Rye*. He waved the book at me as I came through the sliding doors. "Never read this as a kid. Not sure what all the fuss is about. I mean, what kid ever likes his parents?"

"It's about a mental breakdown, really."

"Yeah? Well, I haven't got that far yet." He chucked the book onto the seat. "Walk with me."

We headed toward Government Street. The place wasn't clogged with tourists at this time of year, but the boats in the Inner Harbour were spectacular. No one recognized Wilcox, which was probably a relief for him. We sat down on a bench and talked about which boat we'd sail away on if we could. Then we were silent for a long time.

Eventually Wilcox turned to me and said, "I can't stop thinking about how you killed that song the other night." His stare was intense. "When are you coming to Vancouver?"

As I opened my mouth to answer, Viv's voice echoed in my head.

I'm heading to California with Joe. He's in this great band...

Rob is taking me to NYC. Can you believe it?

You'll be fine, baby girl. Here's a hundred bucks. If you don't have enough, you know where the dumpsters are...

I shook my head until her voice disappeared.

"I hope that doesn't mean you've changed your mind," Wilcox said. Then he leaned in and kissed me.

Chapter Eleven

The muscles in my legs dissolved. There was something intense about the kiss, not at all what I'd expected. Not that I had been expecting anything. "Hey," he said when he pulled back. "I wasn't planning to do that. I should have asked. Sorry."

"It's okay." It was more than okay.

"Well, then." He leaned in and kissed me again. Then he held my face between his hands and stared into my eyes. He sighed deeply. "You might want to talk to Gordon about all the arrangements." But suddenly he seemed distracted. Like he was itching to get away from me. Rain clouds rolled in, and it started to rain—quite heavily. He stood up and walked a few paces before turning around. "You coming?"

I trotted to catch up to him. He walked faster as we crossed Government Street and got closer to the hotel. The band's bus was idling outside the entrance, and gear was piled high beside it. The driver was pitching suitcases, instrument cases and duffels into the hold while the band members walked in circles, having one last cigarette.

"There you are! I need to talk to you," Ronnie said to Wilcox as soon as he saw him. "Hi, Serena," he said.

"Stella," I said.

"Right. Sorry." He pulled Wilcox into the lobby, and I watched them talking intensely. Ronnie was waving his hands around. Wilcox's face was stony.

"Looks like Ronnie and Wilcox are having another one of their disagreements," Gordon said. I stepped back. Any expression I might have read in his eyes was hidden by his mirrored sunglasses. "So have you decided if you're going to come to Vancouver?"

"Yes."

"Should be interesting." Gordon took one last look at the lobby and then climbed onto the bus.

Wilcox stormed out of the lobby and brushed by me without saying anything. Ronnie followed him. My head was spinning. One minute Wilcox was kissing me, and the next minute he was acting like I was invisible.

Was I in some kind of alternate reality?

I went back to my regular life, and before I knew it nearly another week had gone by. Not one word from Viv. She could have been eaten by a piranha for all I knew. I hadn't heard from Wilcox either, but my knees went wobbly every time I remembered the kisses. When I'd told Marnie what had happened, she'd practically fallen over. I had sworn her to secrecy, but the look on her face had made me immediately wonder if I'd made a huge mistake in telling her.

Now it was Friday morning, and I was on the ferry. Max had driven me to the terminal. He'd looked at me hard when he dropped me off. "Keep your head, Stell. We'll see you back here tomorrow. Don't forget Pod has its first gig featuring our first-ever female singer tomorrow night." He'd tapped his temple. "Stay strong." I'd agreed to do a few shows with the band. We'd been practicing. Figuring out the songs. Our gig was booked in a venue downtown where lots of bands had got their first break.

I got off the ferry and hopped on the city bus to downtown Vancouver. I walked to the hotel where Gordon had told me the band was staying. He met me in the lobby and took me upstairs to my room. "I've got another interview set up for you over at the arena at four. A national station. You'll be on the news tonight. Local girl sings again."

"Where's Wilcox?" I needed to see him. He hadn't left my mind all week. Not when I was rehearsing with Pod. Not when I was busking down at the wharf. And especially not when I was lying in bed, looking at his face on my wall.

"At the arena. Go freshen up, and then we'll get you over there so you can do a run-through before your interview."

The place was five times the size of the venue in Victoria. This was a rock concert on steroids. Wilcox waved at me from center stage. He was back to acting the way he had before the kiss. Ronnie stood to one side of him, tuning his bass.

"Stell! Great to see you. Let's do your number right now. Don't be intimidated by the size of the place," Wilcox said. "It's the same thing as last time, only bigger."

My voice broke on the first run-through. Wilcox came up behind me and massaged my shoulders. The tension drained away, and my skin where he was touching me tingled. "One more time."

When the practice was over, Wilcox walked me offstage. "That was great. Just remember to keep the nerves in check. I'll see you tonight." Then he turned and walked back to the stage. For a moment I thought maybe I had imagined the whole kissing incident. Wilcox was definitely acting like it had never happened.

Gordon came to get me ready for the TV interview. Everything was going so fast, my head wouldn't stop spinning. I told the interviewer how great it was singing with Razor. No, I said, I had never imagined this would happen from one YouTube video. Yes, I would like to be a professional singer. Yes, it was all a little surreal.

Then it was showtime. When it was time for my performance, I put everything I had into it. I felt every note, every lyric, like it was part of me. I don't remember if there was applause or not. I needed to talk to Wilcox. I needed to know where I fit. I waited backstage for him to come and find me after the show. When he didn't, I went to his dressing room. The door was open a notch, and I could hear low, angry voices coming from inside.

"What are you playing at?" said a voice it took me a moment to recognize. Ronnie.

"Nothing. Get off my case." It was Wilcox. Then a crash.

"Good. Great. Breaking things is really going to help."

"Like I said. Shut. Up."

"She's sixteen, man. You're thirty. That's jailbait. Is that why you think you can get away with it? Because she won't know any better?" Another crash. I inched closer to the door. I saw Ronnie bend down to pick up a broken bottle.

"You don't know what you're talking about." Wilcox moved into Ronnie's space. They stared at each other intensely.

"Well, I do know this." I watched Ronnie pull Wilcox toward him. They kissed. I felt my mouth where a week ago he'd kissed me. "Stop trying to fight it."

Wilcox didn't shove Ronnie away. After a very long moment, he slumped down onto the couch, his head in his hands. And that told me everything I needed to know.

Where I fit into the picture was pretty clear.

I didn't.

Chapter Twelve

First thing the next morning, I told Gordon I had to leave. "You did real good, kid." He slid his sunglasses onto the top of his head. "It was fun while it lasted."

"Yeah." I wondered if he knew what was going on. The expression on his face gave away nothing.

"You are very talented, kid. You definitely have a future in the biz if you want it. Like I said, I can give you a couple of names. Agents and so on." Despite all his kind words, I could tell that already Gordon's attention had moved on. I was yesterday's news. Not a word about touring in March. He handed me a check. "A token of appreciation. Don't spend it all in one place."

It was for five hundred dollars. "I won't." It would almost pay for half the rent.

The ferry was full of families. The captain came on the PA system to announce that a pod of orcas was passing on the starboard side. I watched them swim by, their dorsal fins like black sails. Everyone, it seemed, had families. Except me.

By the time I got back to the apartment, a wet, black cloud hung over me. I called Max and told him I was sick. That I wouldn't be at the gig that night. He offered to come over, bring me whatever I needed, but I told him not to. I didn't want anyone to pity me.

After I ripped the Razor posters off my wall, I climbed into bed and pulled the covers over my head. I'd always thought I was nothing like Viv. That I would never, ever drop everything to follow a band around. Or fall for a guy in a band. I squirmed at the memory of that kiss and all that I had read into it. At all the stupid hopes I had pinned on it. I cried myself to sleep. When I woke up the sky was heavy with rain. I still hadn't heard a word from Viv. And so much had happened. I'd sung twice with a world-famous band, been kissed by a guy who hadn't figured out who he really was and lost my shot at the big time. My fifteen minutes was up.

One of my notebooks lay open on my desk. I looked over the songs I'd been trying to write over the past few weeks. A line came into my head. *Coming down after the high.* I played with the lyric, thinking how it really explained it all. I worked on it for the rest of the weekend.

On Monday morning I made my way to school, deflated. Kids slammed their locker doors shut. Complained about assignments. Nothing felt the same to me, but to them it was just another Monday. Jared and Marnie came toward me, and Marnie waved but didn't stop to chat. She didn't even ask about the Vancouver show. "Talk to you later, okay?" she said as she went by. I felt even more deflated.

"Hi." I looked up to see Max coming through the front doors. "Feeling better?" he asked.

"I'm sorry about Saturday."

"No worries. There will be other gigs. You look kind of pale. You sure you're okay?"

I nodded because I wasn't sure I could speak.

"I warned you this stuff can mess with your head." Max's face was kind. Kindness is the hardest thing to take. Before I could stop them, tears overflowed. I swiped at them angrily.

"Come with me." Max grabbed my hand. He pulled me out into the cold and steered me away from the school. We ducked into a café and ordered two coffees and two muffins. Then we walked until we reached the steps of the Belfry Theatre. We sat down. "Drink," he said. "It looks like you haven't eaten for a week."

It wasn't far from the truth. The coffee helped. So did the muffin. "Blueberry," I said. "My favorite."

"So, you ready to come back to the band? The guys were bummed you didn't show on Saturday. I had to work hard to convince them you hadn't just bailed because you thought you were too good for us."

"I never thought they would take it like that." I felt terrible. I just hadn't been able to face anything that day.

"They're musicians. They're very sensitive." Max smiled.

"I'm sorry. I really am. The whole thing with Razor did really mess with my head. But you guys are great, and it would be an honor to sing with you."

He sipped his coffee, then glanced at me. He put his cup down on the steps and reached into his backpack. He pulled out my notebook and handed it back to me. "You know those songs you asked me to look at? They're good. I'd like to work on one or two for Pod. How do you feel about that?"

"I never thought they were that good."

"Well, they are."

I took my notebook out of my backpack. "I wrote this one last night." I handed him my new song.

He accepted my gift. "Leave it with me."

I nodded. I liked that. It seemed like a promise.

"Listen up, everybody! Spring is in the air and it's Pod night here at the Cabaret. And we have a new member. Give it up for Stella Connors!"

Max nodded. The opening chords of my song filled the air. I stepped up to the mic. I was going to do it. Sing one of my own songs, on my own terms.

My voice blasted the room. Angry. Sad. Angry again. The band stayed with me, tight and rocking.

I looked out into the audience and there she was. Viv. Just like she said she'd be. Standing at the bar, talking to a guy, barely listening to me. I belted out the chorus. Felt the power in my voice. Felt the room lean forward and take notice.

Yesterday I had come home from school. Viv's duffel was in the hallway. Dirty clothes spilled out onto the floor. Never mind I hadn't heard a word from her since February and now it was April. Never mind that three long months of rehearsing and gigging with Pod were behind me. Never mind that I'd paid the rent, and all the other bills, the whole time she was gone. There she was, lying on the couch, her grimy feet propped against the wall while she smoked a joint. "Hi, baby girl," she said when she saw me. "I'm back."

I knew at that moment that I was never going to get what I wanted from Viv. I tried hard not to mind. I kicked her tangled macramé beach bag out of the way and went to sit down beside her.

"What happened to Javier?" I had asked.

"Who knows? Who cares? Turns out he was too needy."

I had cocked an eyebrow. *He* was too needy? Viv had waved her joint, brushed a tear from her cheek. "I've got options, baby girl." She sniffed and grabbed my hand. "What do we have to eat?" she had asked. I had gone into the kitchen, grabbed a bag of day-old cinnamon buns and handed them to her. She had picked at them with one hand while sniffling and wiping her nose on her tie-dyed T-shirt with the other.

I watched her. For the first time I noticed a strand of white hair. Smile lines beside her eyes stood out white against her tan. Viv. Long Gone Viv. It really didn't matter anymore. Maybe in time I could really believe that.

When I finished the song, the crowd exploded. Max put his arm over my shoulders. Squeezed it like a brother would. And that was okay. This time I was *in* the band, not following it.

For good or for bad, from now on, that was how it was going to be.

I bowed slightly and turned. The next number was one of Pod's.

I stepped into the spotlight and started to sing.

Acknowledgments

Thanks to John for his insights, Dan for his music know-how and the gang who made it all possible—Hilary, Tanya and the amazing team at Orca.

Nancy Belgue is the author of several books for young people, including the popular *Casey Little, Yo-Yo Queen*. Her writing has appeared in magazines in both Canada and the United States. In addition to speaking to children as a visiting author, Nancy has worked as a literary/drama artist with the Learning Through The Arts program and has acted in television commercials, training videos and documentaries. She lives in Kingsville, Ontario.

GIRLS LIKE ME

KRISTIN BUTCHER

9781459820555 PB

Chapter One

The pain comes in waves. So does the blood—so much blood. My once-sky-blue sheets are now ax-murderer red.

There is a knock on my bedroom door. Before I can make myself answer, my mother is beside my bed. "Ed!" she screams. "Call an ambulance!"

I can't wait for it. I pass out, and the first responders arrive without my noticing. I miss the ride to the hospital too—the reckless weaving through the streets, the sirens wailing and lights flashing, the other vehicles diving for the curb to get out of the way. Inside the ambulance, the paramedics do whatever it is paramedics do, and though I am the one they are doing it to, I am unaware.

I don't remember arriving at the hospital either—only the vague blip of lights whizzing past overhead and voices talking around me. I wonder if I'm dying, and then I lose consciousness again.

When I truly wake up, I have to blink the world into focus. I am lying in a hospital bed, looking up at the ceiling. I turn my head and see that my arm is attached to some kind of machine. On my other side, a pouch of clear liquid hangs from a pole. A long, skinny tube snakes its way from it to my wrist.

I'm groggy, and my stomach hurts. I feel like a wrung-out dishrag.

My mother is there. She jumps up from a chair and presses her worried face against mine.

"Oh, Emma. Emma," she says, clutching my hand. Finally she pulls away and looks at me hard. I can tell she is trying to understand.

Then I see my father standing at the end of the bed. He's holding two cardboard cups of coffee. He sets them down on the tray table stretching across my legs and hurries to the other side of the bed. Ignoring the monitor on my finger, he takes my hand in both of his.

"Oh, baby," he says. "Thank god you're all right. Your mother and I have been worried sick."

I smile. At least, I try to. But the muscles in my face have seized up, and nothing much happens. "Sorry," I say. The word comes out as a croak, so I try again. The second effort is no better than the first.

My father pats my hand, as if to say he understands, but I know he doesn't.

"You women and your female troubles," he says awkwardly.

He has no clue.

But my mother does. Though she smiles at my dad's lame joke, her grip on my hand tightens. Oh yeah. She knows.

The doctor keeps me in the hospital overnight, but I am released the next morning. My parents take me home.

I enter my bedroom cautiously, half expecting to see the previous day's horror. But there's not a trace. My mother has taken care of it, and the room is as pristine as it has been my whole life. It looks exactly the same—right down to the blue sheets on the bed. New ones.

The old ones will be in the trash. Not even my mother could clean away that much blood. And she would want all evidence of what happened gone.

It is a quiet day. My parents and I retreat to our corners, avoiding awkward conversation. My mother stays in the kitchen with her pots and pans, ignoring the fact that she's making enough food to feed the neighborhood. My father holes up in his man cave, watching football with the sound turned way down. I hide in my bedroom, pretending to read.

I've just lived through a six-week nightmare, capped off with twenty-four hours of pure hell. Even so, I am still having trouble getting my head around everything. This kind of stuff doesn't happen to girls like me.

Except that it did.

I'm barely three months into eleventh grade, and the year is already unforgettable—for all the wrong reasons.

It started when Jen and I both made the senior girls' volleyball team. The two of us have been joined at the hip since kindergarten—Brownies, gymnastics, tennis lessons, summers at the lake, lemonade stands—we've done all of it together. We even kid around that one day we'll marry twins and have a double wedding. So we kind of expected that if one of us made the team, the other would too.

For a while it was great. The schedule for the senior girls was the same as for the senior boys, so game days were like a big party. After the matches everyone would meet up at a fast-food place for a few laughs before heading home.

Then something happened. Jen and I both fell for Ross Schroeder. He's the power hitter on the boys' volleyball team. And he's in twelfth grade. He has it all—a jock with good looks, smarts and personality. Every girl in school thinks he's hot, so why not Jen and me?

At first we laughed about it. I mean, it figures we would fall for the same guy, right? However, it soon became clear that neither one of us was going to back off. That's when things got a little tense, especially when Ross was around. But the day he picked up the tab for my food at the restaurant, our friendship was over.

Jen and I were standing in line behind him.

"Root beer, not cola—right?" he said to me.

My stomach flipped. I was flattered that he'd noticed what drink I liked. I nodded.

"Fries?"

I smiled and nodded again, reaching into my pocket for money. He shook his head.

"This one's on me, Emma."

"Thanks," I said. I waited for him to ask Jen what she wanted.

When he didn't, I could almost see the wall going up between us. She didn't even sit with Ross and me, and as soon as she was done eating, she left.

Despite having the coolest guy in school all to myself, I felt like a heavy rock had just dropped into my stomach.

"There goes my ride," I said, as I watched Jen's car pull out of the parking lot. "I better call my dad."

"Don't worry about it," Ross said. "I can give you a lift home."

A quiet tap on my bedroom door jerks me out of the memory. I look up from the page I've been staring at ever since I opened the book.

My mother pokes her head into the room. "Supper's on the table," she says. "Lasagna—your favorite." Then her head disappears. But in a second it's back again. "Oh, and Emma, I think it would be best if you stayed home from school tomorrow. Give your body a bit more time to recover." She shrugs. "You know."

I want life to be normal again, and that includes school. So I say, "Honestly, Mom, I'm fine. I'm just a little tired. All I need is a good night's sleep."

She shakes her head. "Missing one day is not going to affect your school-work. I think it's best. You can use the time to book a follow-up appointment with the doctor."

I bite the inside of my lip. Visiting old Dr. Abernathy is the last thing I want to do. I saw how he looked at me in the hospital. The only reason he didn't start preaching right then was because my parents were there. Behind the closed door of his office, I won't be so lucky.

"You need to talk to him," my mother says.

Why? I almost blurt. *What's there to talk about?*

I was pregnant, and now I'm not. I don't even want to think about it, never mind talk about it. Nobody was supposed to find out. But now Dr. Abernathy knows, and so does my mother— even though she hasn't come right out and said anything.

I squeeze my eyes shut and wish myself anywhere but where I am.

When I open them again, I'm still sitting on my bed, and my mother is still watching me.

"Supper's getting cold," she says and heads back to the kitchen.

Bookworm reads.

Welcome, friend!

Can I come in?

Bookworm crawls.

Snow falls.

Bookworm reads.

Everyone, unpack!

Ducks stack.

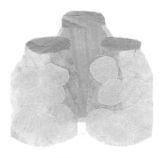

Rabbits snip.

Raccoons tip.

Bookworm reads.

Chipmunks chase.

Rats race.

Bookworm reads.

Bears saw and sand.

Owls draw a plan.

Bookworm

by Molly Coxe

To June and Cathe

Library of Congress Cataloging-in-Publication Data
Coxe, Molly.
Bookworm / by Molly Coxe
  p. cm.—(Road to reading. Mile 1)
Summary: While all the animals help Owl build a house, Bookworm reads, but they
welcome him inside anyway when the snow comes.
ISBN 0-307-26112-3 (pbk.)—ISBN 0-307-46112-2 (GB)
[1. Animals—Fiction. 2. Dwellings—Fiction. 3. Stories in rhyme.] I. Title. II. Series.
PZ8.3.C8395Bo 2000
[E]—dc21   99-87822

A GOLDEN BOOK • New York
Golden Books Publishing Company, Inc. New York, New York 10106

ISBN: 0-307-26112-3 (pbk.)   A MM
ISBN: 0-307-46112-2 (GB)

Dear Parents

Buckle up! You are about to join your child on a very exciting journey. The destination? Independent reading!

Road to Reading will help you and your child get there. The program offers books at five levels, or Miles, that accompany children from their first attempts at reading to successfully reading on their own. Each Mile is paved with engaging stories and delightful artwork.

Getting Started
For children who know the alphabet and are eager to begin reading
• easy words   • fun rhythms   • big type   • picture clues

Reading With Help
For children who recognize some words and sound out others with help
• short sentences   • pattern stories   • simple plotlines

Reading On Your Own
For children who are ready to read easy stories by themselves
• longer sentences   • more complex plotlines   • easy dialogue

First Chapter Books
For children who want to take the plunge into chapter books
• bite-size chapters   • short paragraphs   • full-color art

Chapter Books
For children who are comfortable reading independently
• longer chapters   • occasional black-and-white illustrations

There's no need to hurry through the Miles. Road to Reading is designed without age or grade levels. Children can progress at their own speed, developing confidence and pride in their reading ability no matter what their age or grade.

So sit back and enjoy the ride—every Mile of the way!

Praying with the Hebrew Scriptures

Rejoice and Be Glad!

Franciscan Spiritual Center-West
3300 SE Dwyer Drive Suite 306
Milwaukie, OR 97222-6548

Praying with the Hebrew Scriptures

Rejoice and Be Glad!
Meditations on Fifteen Psalms

Maureena Fritz, NDS

Saint Mary's Press
Christian Brothers Publications
Winona, Minnesota

For my parents, Maura and Simon, who gave to my seven sisters and brothers and to me a thirst for knowledge and the energy to pursue learning;

For my Theresa and Gerard, who already know what our heart and mind yearn for; and

For my Joe, Eileen, Mary, Kathleen, and Frank, whose love and support always encourage me to pursue the grace of Torah study and to make the commitment to share its beauty.

Among those to whom I would like to express my gratitude are my many students at Ecce Homo residence in Jerusalem and my Sisters of Sion at Bin Karem, Israel. Earlier versions of several of these chapters were used in conferences with them and their comments helped me to bring a sharper focus to some of these reflections. It is also a personal pleasure for me to recognize, once again, the support of three friends in New York: Jack Rudin, Edward Arrigoni, and Jack Driscoll, CFC, who continue to support my efforts to promote the spread of God's word in my writing and lecturing.

The publishing team for this book included Carl Koch, FSC, development editor; Joellen Barak Ramer, copy editor; Barbara Bartelson, production editor and typesetter; Sharon Binder, illustrator; Stephan Nagel, art director; *City of Angels* cover photo from an oil painting by David Sharir, courtesy of Pucker Gallery, Boston; pre-press, printing, and binding by the graphics division of Saint Mary's Press.

The acknowledgments continue on page 88.

 Genuine recycled paper with 10% post-consumer waste. Printed with soy-based ink.

Printed in the United States of America

Printing: 9 8 7 6 5 4 3 2

Year: 2003 02 01 00 99 98 97 96 95

ISBN 0-88489-305-7

Contents

Have you not heard his silent steps? He comes, comes, ever comes.

Every moment and every age, every day and every night he comes, comes, ever comes.

Many a song have I sung in many a mood of mind, but all their notes have always proclaimed, "He comes, comes, ever comes."

In the fragrant days of sunny April through the forest path he comes, comes, ever comes.

In the rainy gloom of July nights on the thundering chariot of clouds he comes, comes, ever comes.

In sorrow after sorrow it is his steps that press upon my heart, and it is the golden touch of his feet that makes my joy to shine.

(Rabindranath Tagore, *Collected Poems*, XLV)

Preface

Sing aloud, O daughter Zion;
   shout, O Israel!
Rejoice and exult with all your heart,
   O daughter Jerusalem!

(Zeph. 3:14)

We are made for happiness, for rejoicing. Everything in life is toward that goal. Even tears can lead to jubilation.

The Book of Psalms enables us to wind our way through sorrow to joy, through darkness to light, through death to resurrection. Even in approaching death, when the left hand protests, "How disastrous is this disgrace," the right hand proclaims, "How wonderful is this triumph."

The meditations in this book are arranged around the themes of birth and innocence, coming to maturity, and maturity. The Psalms of Innocence celebrate and direct new beginnings. They proceed from joy to joy and contain the recipe for happiness. They encourage us to sing and rejoice in our unique and special relationship with God. They remind us that intimacy with God is a real possibility.

The Psalms of Protest remind us of pain and frustration, anger and protest. They even challenge God and call God to account. Nevertheless, the terrible struggle with God ends not in separation, but in deep friendship. A new understanding of God leads to self-confidence, security, and song.

The Psalms of Experience celebrate the fruits of the struggle. God is not so much questioned as praised. Stars, moon, sun, plants, animals, birds, children, women, men, and the events of history are all called to praise God. They become the great orchestra of trumpets, lutes, harps, tambourines, strings, pipes, and clashing cymbals that breaks forth into the final crescendo: "Let everything that breathes praise the Lord!"

Maureena Fritz, NDS

Spontaneous Joy:
Psalms of Innocence

Then our mouth was filled with laughter,
and our tongue with shouts of joy.

(Ps. 126:2)

Life is filled with new beginnings. New days, months, and years.
New friends, jobs, situations, and places. New discoveries and insights. New feelings and thoughts. New experiences.

New beginnings evoke excitement, hope, expectation, and
wonder. We may be anxious about how we will handle the new
situation. Risk is involved. What will we say and do? How should
the new be approached? Whatever we may feel, we are marked
by a certain innocence as we enter into newness. After all, we
have never been down the new road before.

No matter how long we have tried to live a life of faith, each
day is a new gift from God. No matter how experienced we are or
how humdrum our lives have become, revelations from God con-
stantly invite our attention.

Does God's word give us any guidelines that lead to happiness? Of course. God offers us guidance and nourishment for going on the journey joyfully. The psalms for meditation in this
section provide divine wisdom. Meditation 1, on Psalm 1, gives
us a guide for the road, a recipe for staying fully alive. Meditations 2 and 3, on Psalms 145 and 146 respectively, remind us
that we must never lose our praise-filled orientation toward life.
As we develop the ability to praise, we increase our capacity to be
in awe of things. Meditation 4, on Psalm 8, deals with empower-
ment and creative action. Meditation 5, on Psalm 131, focuses on
the tenderness of God and the joys of contemplative rest.

Rejoice!
You Are Shown the Way

Psalm 1 is a biblical recipe for happiness. Taking delight in God's word forms the heart of the recipe. Delight in our heart and a smile on our lips please God, for they bring light and warmth to the world. Like a river of living water, delight flowing from the heart refreshes and renews all that it touches. With delight in God's word, doubt gives way to faith, despair to hope, darkness to light, and sadness to joy. Day after day, God invites us to choose life: "I call heaven and earth to witness against you today that I have set before you life and death, blessings and curses. Choose life so that you and your descendants may live" (Deut. 30:19).

Psalm 1

1   Happy are those who do not
        walk in the counsel of the wicked,
    nor stand in the way of sinners,
        nor sit in the seat of the scornful.

2   But their delight is in the Torah of the LORD;
        and on God's Torah they meditate day and night.

3   They are like trees planted by streams of water,
        which yield their fruit in its season.
    Their leaves do not wither;
        in all that they do, they prosper.

4   The wicked are not so,
        but are like chaff that
        the wind drives away.

5 Therefore the wicked will not
     stand in the judgment,
   nor sinners in the congregation of the righteous.

6 For the LORD knows the ways of the righteous
     but the way of the wicked will perish.

Commentary

Psalm 1 has three parts: the first part describes what happiness is *not;* the second part states what happiness *is,* and the final section compares the destiny of the righteous to that of the wicked.

The first part begins in the manner of the Beatitudes, "Happy is the one . . ." The Psalmist then describes that which is *not* happiness. The happy person does not associate with the enemies of life, does not walk, stand, or sit with them. The sequence of these verbs is important. They describe the successive steps in a career of evil. *Walk* refers to one's association with chance acquaintances; *stand* indicates a more fixed relationship; and *sit* implies a permanent relationship.

To be happy, people must not have even chance acquaintance with the wicked who are ungodly and the opposite of the righteous. The wicked willfully and persistently violate the commands of God. To be happy, the righteous should not stand with *sinners,* translated from the Hebrew as "those who miss the mark." Sinners miss the mark because of ignorance and lack of moral strength. The scorners do not know the ways of God, despise piety, and delight in corrupting others. Above all, the righteous should not sit with these. The wicked, the sinners, and the scorners choose death over life.

After telling us what *not* to do if we are to be happy, the Psalmist announces a prescription for happiness: delighting in the Torah, the word of God. God wants to be known and wants us to live in a way conducive to happiness. When we study the Torah, we come to know God and the ways of God. God's word is "a lamp to our feet" (see Ps. 119:105). Authentic study requires that we engage the text, interpret it, react to it, and respond to it. This act of study is revelation; we hear God speaking to us here and now. Study demands time. So the Psalmist reminds us that

11

the happy meditate day and night on God's word because it is their delight and preoccupation.

Studying the Torah rewards us richly. Each hour of study pays us a salary. The Psalmist describes the salary in terms of a tree that brings forth its fruit in season. The fruit is an undiminished sense of well-being, zest for life, hope, faith, and love. Like a tree that remains perennially green, so are those who make the Torah their preoccupation.

Psalm 1 closes by comparing the righteous to deeply rooted trees whose leaves stay green. The leaves of the wicked wither, fall, and scatter like chaff in the wind. The righteous ignore fleeting pleasures in order to study the Torah, so they reap their reward—knowledge and intimacy with God:

> For the LORD knows the ways of the righteous
> But the way of the wicked will perish.
>
> (Ps. 1:6)

Reflections

❑ Reflective writing can lead to interpretation, and interpretation is revelation. Read each of the following reflection questions. Choose one that attracts you. Ponder the question for a moment, and begin writing spontaneously without censoring yourself. This type of writing is a way of listening to God's inspiration coming from your soul.

- Those who are not anchored are like chaff blown about by every kind of wind. What or who is your anchor? What do you cling to in times of trouble? What is it that gives direction to your life?
- Streams of water nourish, and once you find them, you can return to them. What are your streams of water? How is delighting in Bible study like a stream of water for you?
- Who are the wicked, the sinners, and the scorners with whom you should not walk, stand, or sit? Which people would prevent you from being an upright and honest person?
- Jesus ate with sinners and spoke to prostitutes and tax collectors. Are these the worst of all sinners?

12

Torah study and reflection with a partner is an Emmaus experience. Study Psalm 1 and reflect with a partner on one of the following questions:

❏ Recall a time when you felt withered, with little to offer to others. Then remember a time when you felt like a tree planted by living waters. What graces did you receive from both experiences? Write and pray a psalm of your own, thanking God for the graces from both of these moments.

❏ Choose life. The Hebrew text is more faithfully translated as "choose *into* life." Reflect on the difference. What can you do now and tomorrow to choose into life? Draw up a short list of steps you can take to choose life.

❏ Meditate on this story and its meaning for you:

> A hassid [a holy person] complained to the rabbi of Ger: "I have worked and toiled and yet I have not the satisfaction of a master-craftsman who, after twenty years of effort, finds some result of his labours in his work: either it is better than it was at first, or he can do it more quickly. I see nothing at all. Just as I prayed twenty years ago, so I pray today."
>
> The zaddik [leader of the community] answered: "It is taught in Elijah's name: '[Humans] should take the Torah upon [themselves], as the ox takes the yoke and the ass his burden.' You see, the ox leaves his stall in the morning, goes to the field, plows, and is led home, and this happens day after day, and nothing changes with regard to the ox, but the ploughed field bears the harvest." (Martin Buber, *Tales of the Hasidim*, p. 304)

❏ List some of the rewards or salary you received for the time you have just spent on this psalm.

Memory Verse

My "delight is in the Torah of the LORD."

(Ps. 1:2)

13

Rejoice!
God's Love Underlies

Meditation 2 offers another recipe for happiness. Psalm 145 teaches us how to bless and praise God. In Hebrew, the words "bless" and "spring" have the same root. Those who bless are like springs of life-giving water (John 4:14).

Psalm 145 begins with the words of a confident lover—*I* will bless your name for ever and ever. Every day, *I* will bless your name. *I* will praise your name for ever and ever. The psalm continues by declaring in effect that no matter what happens, *I* will sing your praises, and though others proclaim your awesome deeds, *I* will go further and declare your greatness in everything that you do.

Psalm 145

1 I will extol you, my God and King,
    and bless your name forever and ever.
2 Every day I will bless you,
    and praise your name forever and ever.
3 Great is the LORD, and greatly to be praised;
    his greatness is unsearchable.

4 One generation shall laud your works to another,
    and shall declare your mighty acts.
5 On the glorious splendor of your majesty,
    and on your wondrous works, I will meditate.
6 The might of your awesome deeds shall be proclaimed,
    and I will declare your greatness.
7 They shall celebrate the fame of your abundant goodness,
    and shall sing aloud of your righteousness.

8   The LORD is gracious and merciful,
        slow to anger and abounding in steadfast love.
9   The LORD is good to all,
        and his compassion is over all that he has made.

10 All your works shall give thanks to you, O LORD,
        and all your faithful shall bless you.
11 They shall speak of the glory of your kingdom,
        and tell of your power,
12 to make known to all people your mighty deeds,
        and the glorious splendor of your kingdom.
13 Your kingdom is an everlasting kingdom,
        and your dominion endures throughout all
            generations.

    The LORD is faithful in all his words,
        and gracious in all his deeds.
14 The LORD upholds all who are falling,
        and raises up all who are bowed down.
15 The eyes of all look to you,
        and you give them their food in due season.
16 You open your hand,
        satisfying the desire of every living thing.
17 The LORD is just in all his ways,
        and kind in all his doings.
18 The LORD is near to all who call on him,
        to all who call on him in truth.
19 He fulfills the desire of all who fear him;
        he also hears their cry, and saves them.
20 The LORD watches over all who love him,
        but all the wicked he will destroy.

21 My mouth will speak the praise of the LORD,
        and all flesh will bless his holy name forever and
            ever.

Commentary

Psalm 145 is unique in that it praises God for both good and bad things—nothing is omitted. Those who recite it three times daily in the synagogue are assured of inheriting the world to come. After all, how can anyone be lost who praises God for all things morning, afternoon, and night?

The verses follow the sequence of the letters of the Hebrew alphabet and use the entire range of human sounds to praise God. The symphony of sounds climaxes in a final announcement that all flesh will bless God's holy name forever and ever.

The opening verses set the mood for the whole psalm:

> I will extol you, *my* God and King,
>> I will bless your name *forever* and ever.
> *Every day* I will bless you,
>> and bless your name *forever* and ever.
>
> (vv. 1–2, emphasis added)

These words are firm, sure, strong expressions of faith in and love of God.

Praise and blessings are made with full knowledge of the joy and sadness, health and sickness, victory and failure in life. In verses six and seven, "they" praise God for "awesome deeds" and "abundant goodness"—that is, for success and plenty, but not for pain and suffering. On the other hand, in verse six, "I" declares God's "greatness" in all things. With awareness that God's love covers both reward and punishment, and despite sickness, starvation, war, and death, the "I" announces:

> The LORD is gracious and merciful. . . .
> The LORD is good to all. . . .
> The LORD upholds all who are falling,
>> and raises up all who are bowed down. . . .

To "they" who would only praise God in the good times, Rabbi Akiba concludes that the "I" replies:

> Ye shall not behave towards Me in the manner in which others behave toward their deities. When good comes to them they honor their gods. . . . But when evil comes to them they curse their gods. . . . But ye, if I bring good upon you,

give ye thanks, and when I bring suffering upon you, give ye thanks. (Jacob Lauterbach, trans., *Mekilta De-Rabbi Ishmael*, vol. 2, p. 277)

Conscious that God's sovereignty is unsearchable, "I's" answer might be summarized this way: I cannot hope to understand your ways, yet I know that you are good to all. You have compassion for all creation. You uphold all who are falling and raise up all who are bowed down. You open your hand, satisfying the desire of every living thing. You are near to all who call upon you in earnest. You are just in all your ways and kind in all your doings.

Despite apparent contradictions, the Psalmist believes that God is creator and sovereign of the universe. Nothing exists apart from God. Suffering and evil are all part of the divine plan of love. Giving praise and blessing acknowledges God's overwhelming love for us. How could anyone *not* be happy in the face of such compassionate love?

Reflections

❑ Look back over your week. Praise God for the happy moments that were special to you. Praise God for the moments that were difficult, too.

❑ While you ponder the holy word, God is present to you and speaks to you. Ask that you may hear the divine voice as you engage the text through reflection. Meditate on one or both of these passages, and either discuss them with someone or write in your journal about them:

- It is difficult to see the hand of God where there is pain and evil. Consider the Crucifixion of Jesus. Was Jesus' Crucifixion part of the plan of God? In the garden after the Last Supper, Jesus told Peter: "'Put your sword back into its sheath. Am I not to drink the cup that the Father has given me?'" (John 18:11) Do you think your sufferings are part of God's plan? Can you cling to God despite feeling forsaken?
- Read the story of Joseph in Gen. 37:12–28. Ponder Joseph's sufferings and the feelings he had when he was thrown into the pit and sold into slavery in Egypt. Were Joseph's sufferings part of God's plan? Even in the ashes of life, hot coals burn. Faith

can find them. Try looking for sparks in some of the most un-
likely places. Recite verses 1 and 2 of Psalm 145 several times.
Stay with verse 6. Let its meaning sink into you as you say it
while reflecting on Joseph in the pit and Jesus on the cross.

❏ The following story is one example of how God feeds the
hungry:

At the beginning of the sixteenth century, a man named Jacobo and his wife, Esperanza, expelled from Spain, settled in
S'fat in the North of Israel. Since Jacobo knew only Spanish,
he never fully understood what went on in synagogue. One
Shabbat he heard the Torah verses from Leviticus 24:5–6 in
which the Children of Israel are instructed to give God
twelve loaves of challah in the ancient wilderness tabernacle
before the Sabbath. He came home full of excitement, "Esperanza! God likes challah for Shabbat and you bake the best
challah in the world. Next Friday bake twelve loaves and we
can bring them to the synagogue for God."

So Esperanza baked her best challah, kneading her good
intentions into the dough. Friday afternoon, when no one
was around, the two brought the twelve challahs to the synagogue, arranged them neatly in the ark, said *"Buen apetito"*
to God, closed the ark and left, very happy. A few minutes
later the janitor came in with his broom. "Dear God," he
said as he stood before the ark, "My children are starving. I
need a miracle." He opened the ark and, finding the challahs
inside, he smiled. He had believed that God would provide.

The next morning when the rabbi opened the ark during services, Esperanza and Jacobo saw immediately that
God had eaten every loaf. They winked at each other with
satisfaction. And so this continued week after week, year after year. Esperanza baked, the janitor and his family ate.

Thirty years passed. One Friday, Esperanza stood before
the ark and said, "God, I'm sorry about the lumps in the
challah. I'm getting old and my fingers don't work as well as
they used to. I hope you enjoy them anyway."

At that moment, the old rabbi of the synagogue appeared and grabbed Esperanza and Jacobo by the collar.
"What are you doing, you fools?" he cried.

"We are giving God his challahs."

"Don't you know that God doesn't eat?"

"You may be a rabbi, but there are some things you don't know. God most certainly *does* eat. In thirty years he has never left behind a crumb."

"Let's hide in the back of the synagogue and see what really happens to your challahs," said the rabbi.

A few minutes later the janitor came in. "Dear God, I don't like to complain, but your challahs have been getting a bit lumpy lately. Still, it's keeping my family alive." He reached into the ark to get his challahs and the rabbi appeared and said, "Stop, you terrible man. . . . God does not have a body. He doesn't bake challah and he doesn't eat challah."

At this, the janitor, Jacobo, and Esperanza all began to cry. The good couple was crying because they had merely wanted to serve God. The janitor was crying because he suspected this meant no more challahs. At that moment the great kabbalist Isaac Luria entered the room.

He turned to the old rabbi. "You must go home immediately and make sure your will is in order. Thirty years ago your time had come to die, but the Angel of Death was called off because God was having so much fun watching what went on in your synagogue. Now it is over, and you will be buried this week, before the Sabbath begins."

Then he turned to the weeping couple and the janitor. "Now that you know who has been eating your challahs, who has been baking your challahs, you must continue to bake them and eat them anyway. Jacobo and Esperanza must bring them every week directly to the janitor. And you must all believe with perfect faith that it is God who bakes and God who takes and that God is no less present in your lives." (Nancy Fuchs-Kreimer, *Cross Currents*, vol. 42, no. 2 [Summer 1992], pp. 212–213)

The good couple, thinking they were giving to God, were giving to the poor; the janitor thought he was receiving from God. Were they correct in their thinking? Meditate on this.

Reread the story and note how the Torah ark is the center of all the giving. What does this say about the word of God as nourishment? How do you let it feed your soul?

Memory Verse

Every day I will bless you,
    and praise your name forever and ever.

(Ps. 145:2)

Rejoice!
Everywhere Divinity

Psalm 146 teaches us that happiness is a by-product of praise, not the reason for praise. If we know with our head *and* heart that God is beyond and within all things, we possess the foundation stone of wisdom. Our song in response will be: "I will praise God now and to the last bit of my ebbing strength."

Psalm 146

1   Praise the LORD!
   Praise the LORD, O my soul!
2   I will praise the LORD as long as I live;
      I will sing praises to my God all my life long.

3   Do not put your trust in princes,
      in mortals, in whom there is no help.
4   When their breath departs, they return to the earth;
      on that very day their plans perish.

5   Happy are those whose help is the God of Jacob,
      whose hope is in the LORD their God,
6   who made heaven and earth,
      the sea, and all that is in them;
   who keeps faith forever;
7   who executes justice for the oppressed;
   who gives food to the hungry.

   The LORD sets the prisoners free;
8   the LORD opens the eyes of the blind.
   The LORD lifts up those who are bowed down;
   The LORD loves the righteous.

9   The LORD watches over the strangers;
        He upholds the orphan and the widow,
        but the way of the wicked he brings to ruin.

10 The LORD will reign forever,
        your God, O Zion, for all generations.
        Praise the LORD!

Commentary

Psalms 146 through 150 begin and end with "Praise the Lord," or "Alleluia," which summarize the content of each psalm. For the faithful, "Alleluia" is the beginning, the middle, and the end of life.

The basis for the "Alleluia" in Psalm 146 is that God is the God of history and the God of creation: "Happy are those whose help is the God of Jacob, whose hope is in the LORD their God, who made heaven and earth" (vv. 5–6).

Psalm 146 begins with a command to the whole of creation to "Praise the Lord!" The second command is addressed to the self, "Praise the Lord, O my soul." The soul responds "I will—as long as I live in all that I do."

The foundation stone of wisdom is to know that "the LORD is God in heaven above and on the earth beneath; there is no other" (Deut. 4:39). This Creator is God of the universe and Lord of the entire world. Nothing moves without divine permission. Nothing is without God. So when we contemplate God's creations and wondrous deeds, we obtain a glimpse of God's infinite, incomparable wisdom. Wonder draws us to love and glorify God.

In light of God's supreme wisdom and love, the Psalmist warns us not to trust in the slippery promises of human leaders and other mortals. The prophet Jeremiah reminds us that God is truth (Jer. 10:10). All other truths are relative.

The firm conviction that God is Creator and Lord of history provides the optimal vantage point from which to appreciate the canvas of life with its good and evil, darkness and light. Without faith, we see myopically, like a person who stands too close to a painting. With the eyes of faith—despite wars, floods, hunger, and death—the Psalmist proclaims:

The LORD sets the prisoners free;
The LORD opens the eyes of the blind.
The LORD lifts up those who are bowed down;
The LORD loves the righteous.
The LORD watches over the strangers.

Note that each line begins with "the LORD" written in capital letters. *LORD* is a substitute word for *Yahweh* (spelled *YHWH*), the name of God revealed to Moses in the burning bush. Yahweh refers specifically to God's attribute of mercy:

"The LORD, the LORD,
a God merciful and gracious,
slow to anger,
and abounding in steadfast love and faithfulness"

(Exod. 34:6–7)

The name *God* stands for justice. It is included as an attribute of mercy because God's justice is also part of God's mercy.

The Lord of mercy and justice sets the prisoners free, opens blind eyes, raises up the lowly, loves the upright, and watches over pilgrims, widows, and orphans. In justice, the wicked will be brought to ruin while the hungry will be given food, the prisoners will be set free, and widows and orphans will be uplifted.

The psalm ends joyfully, as it began, "Alleluia," or "Praise the LORD!"

Reflections

❏ The foundation of all wisdom is knowing that the Creator, the Unbegotten, brought everything into being. Slowly and prayerfully repeat, "The LORD is God in heaven above and on the earth beneath; there is no other" (Deut. 4:39).

❏ Go for a walk. Gaze out your window. Or recall in your memory a special place in nature. As you attend to creation, pray repeatedly: "Praise the Lord. Praise the Lord, O my soul!"

❑ During your work day, pray this line over and over: "The Lord, the Lord, a God merciful and gracious, slow to anger, and abounding in steadfast love and faithfulness." Make note of any effects on your feelings and actions after using this prayer.

❑ Verse 2, "I will sing praises to my God all my life long" has also been translated as "with the little I have left." The "little I have left" can refer to the little bit of good found within a person even in the midst of sinfulness. Finding this "little bit of good" is like finding "sparks" of goodness. What are some of your sparks of goodness, small acts of kindness that you might overlook? Do an examination of your recent past for these sparks and thank God for them.

❑ How can you be a spark of hope for others or ignite sparks of hope in others? Inventory your relationships for these opportunities.
Then ask for the grace you need to spark hope.

❑ Reflect on your limitations, wounds, and weaknesses. For each of them, say "I will praise you with the little I have left."

❑ In imitation of verses 7–9 ("The LORD sets the prisoners free," and so on) write five sentences about the great things God does in your life. Begin each sentence with, "The Lord" and then state the gift. Tell someone of these five gifts.

❑ Ponder this story of mercy and justice from the Talmud, a book containing all the teachings of the Hebrew Bible concerning human life in all its aspects:

> A story is told of a certain man who descended from Upper Galilee and was engaged by an individual in the South for three years. On the eve of the Day of Atonement he requested him, "Give me my wages that I may go and support my wife and children." "I have no money," answered he. "Give me produce," he demanded. "I have none," he replied. "Give me land."—"I have none." "Give me cattle."—"I have none." "Give me pillows and bedding."—"I have none." [The worker] slung his things behind him and went home with a sor-

24

rowful heart. After the Festival his employer took his wages in his hand together with three laden asses, one bearing food, another drink, and the third various sweetmeats, and went to his house. After they had eaten and drunk, he gave him his wages. Said he to him, "When you asked me, 'Give me my wages,' and I answered you, 'I have no money,' of what did you suspect me?" "I thought, 'Perhaps you came across cheap merchandise and had purchased it therewith.'" "And when you requested me, 'Give me cattle' and I answered, 'I have no cattle,' of what did you suspect me?" "I thought 'They may be hired to others.'" "When you asked me, 'Give me land,' and I told you, 'I have no land,' of what did you suspect me?" "I thought, 'Perhaps it is leased to others.'" "And when I told you, 'I have no produce,' of what did you suspect me?" "I thought, 'Perhaps they are not tithed.'" "And when I told you, 'I have no pillows or bedding,' of what did you suspect me?" "I thought, 'Perhaps he has sanctified all his property to Heaven.'" . . . "It was even so; I vowed away all my property because of my son Hyrcanus, who would not occupy himself with the Torah, but when I went to my companions in the South they absolved me of all my vows. And as for you, just as you judged me favourably, so may the Omnipresent judge you favourably." (H. Freedman, trans., and I. Epstein, ed., *Shabbath*, p. 127b)

In Psalm 146, the name for God implies mercy. In the story, the employee shows merciful judgment on his employer. How do you judge others? Is there someone that you have judged harshly? If so, how can you make amends or ignite a spark of hope in this person?

❑ Slowly pray these words attributed to Saint Francis of Assisi:

Lord, make me an instrument of your peace.
Where there is hatred, let me sow love;
Where there is injury, pardon;
Where there is doubt, faith;
Where there is despair, hope;
Where there is darkness, light;
And where there is sadness, joy.

Memory Verse

Praise the LORD, O my soul!

(Ps. 146:1)

Rejoice!
You Are Wonderfully Unique

Humanity, fully alive, is the glory of God. Among all of God's works, the human race stands at the pinnacle of creation: "noble in reason, how infinite in faculties, in form and moving how express and admirable, in action how like an angel, in apprehension how like a god; the beauty of the world; the paragon of animals" (Shakespeare, *Hamlet*, act II, sc. ii). Psalm 8 proclaims God's majesty, and then invites us to celebrate the marvel of our humanity, so "fearfully and wonderfully made" (Ps. 139:14).

Psalm 8

1   O LORD, our Sovereign,
     how majestic is your name in all the earth!

    You have set your glory above the heavens.
2   Out of the mouths of babes and infants
    you have founded a bulwark because of your foes,
     to silence the enemy and the avenger.

3   When I look at your heavens, the work of your fingers,
     the moon and the stars that you have established;
4   what are human beings that you are mindful of them,
     mortals that you care for them?

5   Yet you have made them a little lower than God,
     and crowned them with glory and honor.
6   You have given them dominion over the works of your
     hands,
     you have put all things under their feet,
7   all sheep and oxen,
     and also the beasts of the field,

8   the birds of the air, and the fish of the sea,
       whatever passes along the paths of the seas.

9   O LORD, our Sovereign,
       how majestic is your name in all the earth!

Commentary

Psalm 8 is a lyric of praise to God, but also a lyric of praise of the human person, the manifestation of God's glory par excellence.

The opening and closing sentences are the same and provide the framework for the psalm: "O Lord, our Sovereign, how majestic is your name in all the earth!" All the intervening verses attribute the glory of creation to God: *your* name, *your* glory, *your* heavens, *your* fingers, *your* hands; it is *you* who are mindful, *you* who care for them, and so on. Overwhelmed by the majesty of the moon and stars, the Psalmist proclaims God's sovereignty.

Verses 2–5 describe the special work of God's hands, the human person. God found expression for the divine self in the creation of humanity. From the glory of the heavens, the Psalmist's gaze turns towards children. Compared to the silent witness of the universe, these "babes and infants" with their powers of thought and speech outstrip even the grandeur of the galaxies. The Psalmist exclaims, "Out of the mouths of babes and infants you have founded a bulwark because of your foes, to silence the enemy and the avenger" (v. 2). God uses the speech of children to invoke wonder that overcomes scorners and scoffers.

Whether a person is young or old, male or female, that person is a metaphor of God's glory. Shakespeare proclaims "what a piece of work is a man!" (*Hamlet,* act II, sc. ii) The Psalmist is just as eloquent. And there is more than speech to the human creature. At the beginning of Creation, God said, "Let us make humankind in our image, according to our likeness" (Gen. 1:26). No such declaration was made concerning the sun and the moon, the heavens and the earth.

The prophet Isaiah uses another image to remind the people of Israel about the blessedness of humanity: "Look to the rock from which you were hewn, and to the quarry from which you were dug" (Isa. 51:1). God took stone from the quarry of the di-

vine self and fashioned human beings from it. And thus, the presence of God exists in each human. Humans are a divine gem dug from the quarry of God. The gem does not always shine out to the world. Doubt and despair hide the light, and sin can even bury the gem. Nevertheless, whether we can see the gem glowing in the face of another person or not, God dwells in that person.

God gives humanity the sacred task of being holy as God is holy and of being co-creators, co-redeemers, co-revealers with God to the world.

Reflections

❑ God created each of us as unique manifestations of the sacred. In harmony with your breathing, pray verse 5: "You have . . . crowned them with glory and honor."

Then calmly reflect on the ways in which you manifest God's goodness, mercy, hope, and joy to other people. Honor God's gifts to you by honoring your unique virtues.

❑ Reflect upon and pray with this text: "Look to the rock from which you were hewn" (Isa. 51:1).
- Can you believe that you are a rock from the quarry that is God?
- If you really believe that you are a rock from the quarry of God, what changes can take place in your self-image?
- What changes do you want to make in your life to reflect the fact that you are made in God's image?

❑ If you admit that God has given you and all people "dominion over the works of [God's] hands," what needs your loving attention? God gives you power to do good, to build the Reign of God. Embrace the power, and challenge yourself with these questions:
- As co-creator, how can you improve the plot of earth you now inhabit?
- As co-redeemer, who needs your attention? Who needs to be healed? comforted? delivered?
- As co-revealer, God's revelation depends upon your fidelity to spread the holy word. What can you do today to spread the Good News?

❏ Saint Paul quotes Psalm 8 in several places: Heb. 2:6–10; Eph. 1:22; and 1 Cor. 15:25–27. Examine how the psalm is applied to Jesus. How does it apply to you?

❏ As you go about your day, or through the use of your imagination, when you see people of each age, pray the words from Psalm 8:
- For a child: "Out of the mouths of babes and infants comes wisdom."
- For a youth: "You have been made a little lower than God."
- For a mature person: "You have been given dominion over the works of Creation."
- For an elder: "You have been crowned with glory and honor."

❏ Look at yourself in the mirror and address the words of the psalm to yourself:
- "Out of a childlike person, you, O God, silence the enemy."
- "You, Lord, have made me a little lower than yourself."
- "You have given me dominion over the works of Creation."
- "You have crowned me with glory and honor."
Repeat these phrases. When one of them speaks to you, stay with it.

❏ Consider the gift of speech and the power of the tongue. By a word, Jesus raised Lazarus from the tomb. By a word of slander three people are harmed—the speaker, the spoken to, and the spoken of. The power of the tongue is so great that God placed the tongue behind two "doors"—the lips and the teeth. Examine your speech. Are you speaking the word of God? Or do you often speak lies, spread rumors, or cut with your tongue? Ask God for the graces you need to be a voice for God.

Memory Verse

[Lord], you have made [me] a little lower than [yourself] and crowned [me] with glory and honor.

(Ps. 8:5)

Rejoice!
God Is Motherly Love

Psalm 131 is a tender prayer and a beautiful love poem. The Psalmist rejoices in the complete happiness that occurs when the soul finds peace with God like a weaned child on its mother's breast.

Psalm 131

1   O LORD, my heart is not lifted up,
     my eyes are not raised too high;
   I do not occupy myself with things
     too great and too marvelous for me.
2   But I have calmed and quieted my soul,
     like a weaned child with its mother,
     my soul is like the weaned child that is with me.

3   O Israel, hope in the LORD
     from this time on and forevermore.

Commentary

The Bible frequently describes God's motherly love for us. God conceives human beings, becomes pregnant, gives birth, nourishes, guards, and cares for humanity. In the opening sentences of Genesis, God's spirit, *Ruah,* hovers over the egg of primeval chaos as a mother bird hovers over her nest. In the Exodus story, God is compared to a mother eagle who carries her young to freedom on her strong wings (19:4).

The image of God's protecting love as a mother bird's wings appears in many psalms.

Guard me as the apple of your eye;
    hide me in the shadow of your wings,
from the wicked who despoil me,
    my deadly enemies who surround me.

(Ps. 17:8–9)

Let me abide in your tent forever,
    find refuge under the shelter of your wings.

(Ps. 61:4)

Other images of God's womanly love appear in the Bible:

- God is a weaver who knits together new life:

    For it was you who formed my inward parts;
        you knit me together in my mother's womb.

(Ps. 139:13)

- God is a midwife who aids in the birthing process:

    Yet it was you who took me from the womb;
        you kept me safe on my mother's breast.

(Ps. 22:9)

- God is a scrub woman:

    Purge me with hyssop, and I shall be clean;
        wash me, and I shall be whiter than snow.

(Ps. 51:7)

A frequently occurring scriptural image is of God as mother. When Moses is frustrated with the rebellious Israelites in the desert, he accuses God of neglecting the people God birthed:

"Why have I not found favor in your sight, that you lay the burden of all this people on me? Did I conceive all this people? Did I give birth to them, that you should say to me, 'Carry them in your bosom, as a nurse carries a sucking child,' to the land that you promised on oath to their ancestors?" (Num. 11:11–12)

In one of the last songs ascribed to Moses before he dies, he warns the Israelites to be faithful to God because in the past they were not:

You were unmindful of the Rock that bore you,
    you forgot the God who gave you birth.

(Deut. 32:18)

God will comfort the people "as a mother comforts her child
. . ." (Isa. 66:13). As a mother can never forget the child of her
womb, neither can God:

Can a woman forget her nursing child,
    or show no compassion for the child of her womb?
Even these may forget,
    yet I will not forget you.

(Isa. 49:15)

God's womanly love is present both at the beginning of Creation and throughout the course of history, even at the final redemption. When the fullness of time has come, in the anguished pain of a woman in labor, God will give birth to the new world order.

For a long time I have held my peace,
    I have kept still and restrained myself;
now I will cry out like a woman in labor,
    I will gasp and pant.

(Isa. 42:14)

These maternal images of God help us to understand both the journey to and the place at which the Psalmist has arrived: resting contentedly in the arms of mother God. The poet has found the one thing that brings him happiness.

Of course, the poet did not arrive here without struggle. He tells us simply, "I have calmed and quieted my soul." How many battles the poet fought against pride and arrogance, how many youthful dreams were thwarted, we can only guess. Here the Psalmist has found the true center and, in that center, the true self.

At the center, the Psalmist finds the peace of Sabbath. The word *Sabbath,* another name given to God, is feminine in Hebrew and means *shalom,* or *peace.* That is to say, the name of God, upon whose breast the poet reclines, is Sabbath or shalom.

The Psalmist ends by inviting the larger community into a similar communion with God:

O Israel, hope in the LORD
from this time on and forevermore.

(Ps. 131:3)

Reflections

❑ Calm and quiet your soul like the Psalmist. Sit quietly but alertly. Close your eyes and breathe deeply and slowly. After you have relaxed, pray with each inhalation the word *Mother*, and with each exhalation, *God*. If distractions or other thoughts enter, just acknowledge them and let them go. Pray this way for ten to twenty minutes.

❑ Paint, draw, or watercolor a circular symbolic representation or mandala of your images of God as womanly love for you. Let the act of creating be your psalm of praise.

❑ Write a litany of your fears, worries, disappointments. Then after each one, write "Hope in the Lord." Pray your litany over several days. As you pray, imagine God's motherly love for you.

❑ Jesus described his love as maternal caring, as "a hen gathers her brood under her wings" (Matt. 23:37). Saint Anselm of Canterbury used this image and composed the following prayer:

But you too, good Jesus, are you not also a mother?
Are you not a mother who like a hen gathers her chicks
    beneath her wings? . . .
And you, my soul, dead in yourself,
run under the wings of Jesus your mother
and lament your griefs under his feathers.
Ask that your wounds may be healed
and that, comforted, you may live again.
Christ, my mother, you gather your chickens under your
    wings;
This dead chicken of yours puts himself under those
    wings. . . .

34

Warm your chicken, give life to your dead one, justify your
sinner.

(Benedicta Ward, trans.,
Prayers and Meditations of Saint Anselm, pp. 153–156)

Pray this prayer with Anselm. Imagine yourself warmed, given
life, and justified by Jesus' motherly love. Use the prayer when
you are afraid, anxious, or confused.

❑ The word *sabbath* implies peace, harmony, contentment.
When the word is addressed to God, God is Sabbath, God is
shalom. Conduct an examen of consciousness about your obser-
vance of Sabbath:

■ How do I keep the Sabbath holy?
■ Could I observe the Sabbath in such a way that I could make
  my life more peaceful, my relationships more intimate, my life
  more focused on the will of God?
■ How am I Sabbath for other people?
■ Whose presence in my life brings Sabbath or shalom?

❑ Ask mother God for healing of the bodily and spiritual
wounds that hurt you right now.

Memory Verse

But I have calmed and quieted my soul,
like a weaned child with its mother.

(Ps. 131:2)

Finding Peace in Pain: Psalms of Protest

O LORD, why do you cast me off?
  Why do you hide your face from me?

(Ps. 88:14)

God never promised that we would go through life with no difficulty. Growth involves struggle. Life tests those who have moral strength to endure. Life tests those who become towering examples of courage and hope to others: Abraham, Sarah, Job, Ruth, Jesus, and Mary, Jesus' mother.

We may prefer to numb ourselves to pain or to pretend that suffering does not exist. We may choose to believe that we can go from strength to strength, from less to more. But in the end, death stops for us too.

The psalms that follow deal with pain, abandonment, loss of God's presence, loss of friends, loss of meaning, exile, and bafflement at the ways of God. In meditations 6 and 7, on Psalms 13 and 86 respectively, something has gone terribly wrong, and God is blamed for what has happened. Stubbornly, the speaker in the first meditation waits for God's answer. In the latter meditation, the speaker clings to his faith in God. In meditations 8 and 9, on Psalms 79 and 137, the worst has happened: war, annihilation, and displacement. Through a tenacious clinging to God, the people survive as a nation. A new, radical understanding of God develops in their suffering: God suffers with the people. Meditation 10, on Psalm 51, deals with the pain and slavery caused by sin and the new life and joy available in repentance.

The psalms that follow require courage and a willingness to look at pain, suffering, and disorientation in life. They are for those whose faith undergoes the test of Abraham and Sarah (Genesis 22), the test of Job (Job 1–2), and the test of Mary at the foot of the cross (John 19:25). They are for those who in their determination to be faithful to God are ready to challenge God, to question God, to demand answers in the manner of Job.

How Long, O LORD?

In this psalm, something has gone terribly wrong. In great anguish, the Psalmist lays the full blame upon God, makes four harsh accusations against God, issues three terse demands, gives three reasons why God should grant the demands, and then waits until God answers. When God does answer, the Psalmist's confidence in God and self are renewed and deepened.

Psalm 13

1   How long, O LORD? Will you forget me forever?
         How long will you hide your face from me?
2   How long must I bear pain in my soul,
         and have sorrow in my heart all day long?
     How long shall my enemy be exalted over me?

3   Consider and answer me, O LORD my God!
         Give light to my eyes, or I will sleep the sleep of death,
4   and my enemy will say, "I have prevailed";
         my foes will rejoice because I am shaken.

5   But I trusted in your steadfast love;
         my heart shall rejoice in your salvation.
6   I will sing to the LORD,
         because he has dealt bountifully with me.

Commentary

The speaker in this psalm is in great pain, but refuses to take any personal blame or guilt for what has happened. God is at fault.

The Psalmist knows that nothing happens without divine approval. In four statements, one after the other, the speaker accuses God of forgetting him, hiding from him, allowing him to suffer, and letting his enemies have the upper hand. If God had not gone into hiding, these afflictions would not have happened.

After an explosion of accusation and frustration, the speaker makes three demands of God: consider, answer, and give light. Aware that the situation is beyond personal coping skills, the petitioner's demands become pleas for help. The pleas melt the petitioner's heart. "O Lord" in verse 1 becomes "O Lord, my God." The first outbreak of anger allows the intimacy with God to emerge through the plea.

For each plea, the petitioner offers a reason why God should act—"lest I die . . . lest my enemy say . . . lest my foes rejoice." If any of these things happen, God's glory will be diminished because what happens to God's beloved, happens to God. In other words, "Lord, you don't look so good if I look so bad."

With the situation put squarely in God's lap, the speaker can now wait indefinitely. In verses 5 and 6, the situation has changed dramatically. The speaker joyously proclaims a renewed and deepened commitment to God: "I trusted . . . my heart shall rejoice . . . I will sing," and all because God has "dealt bountifully with me." God's help will come.

The power of such honest, emotional speech is cathartic. It cleanses the speaker of self-recriminations. It also empowers the sufferer and gives the strength to wait it out. In time, the speaker comes to know God's love and graciousness in all that has happened. Although the poem is short, the time span and the journey are long. Nevertheless, the struggle ends in song and gratitude.

Reflections

❑ Write your own story of grievances, unjust sufferings, and feelings of abandonment in the format of this psalm.
■ Begin each grievance with: How long, O Lord? . . .
■ Then make three demands of God, using in turn the words "Consider . . . , Answer . . . , Give light. . . ."

- Close with three statements of a new understanding and deepened commitment to God.

❏ When suffering and loss assail us, we need to express our pain, our suffering, our loss and not repress them lest they become ulcers, back pains, migraines, or we transfer our frustration onto others. Think of a time when you felt you were treated unfairly. Speak out to God, describing the details of the event. Speak until you find some light and consolation.

❏ Read Gen. 18:22–33. From this story we learn that humans may legitimately question God's behavior. Like Abraham, we need not surrender our own sense of justice; we remain free to accept or reject the divine judgment, although we will have to submit to it in the end. Plead with God on behalf of a situation. Note that Abraham did not plead merely for the innocent, but through the merit of the few righteous he prayed for the sinners as well.

❏ Read Num. 20:9–12 and Matt. 8:5–13. Note the power of speech in both situations. In one, speech brings water out of the rock; in the other, it heals. Reflect again on Psalm 13, noting how the words change the poet's own disposition. Pray for waters that will give life to a deadening situation in your life. Pray for healing of some wound that festers inside you.

❏ Sing a hymn of thanksgiving for the bounty of God's mercy to you.

Memory Verse

Consider and answer me, O LORD.

(Ps. 13:3)

40

When Will You Show Your Face?

Insolent people and a band of ruffians who have no fear of God have made life miserable for the Psalmist, but the Psalmist finds refuge by making the problem into *God's* problem. The Psalmist is so boldly trustful and sure of God that God cannot refuse to assume the Psalmist's difficulties.

Psalm 86

1 Incline your ear, O LORD, and answer me,
      for I am poor and needy.
2 Preserve my life, for I am devoted to you;
      save your servant who trusts in you.
3 You are my God; be gracious to me, O Lord,
      for to you do I cry all day long.
4 Gladden the soul of your servant,
      for to you, O Lord, I lift up my soul.
5 For you, O Lord, are good and forgiving,
      abounding in steadfast love to all who call on you.
6 Give ear, O LORD, to my prayer;
      listen to my cry of supplication.
7 In the day of my trouble I call on you,
      for you will answer me.

8 There is none like you among the gods, O Lord,
      nor are there any works like yours.
9 All the nations you have made shall come
      and bow down before you, O Lord,
      and shall glorify your name.
10 For you are great and do wondrous things;
      you alone are God.

11   Teach me your way, O LORD,
      that I may walk in your truth;
      give me an undivided heart to revere your name.
12   I give thanks to you, O Lord my God, with my whole
      heart,
      and I will glorify your name forever.
13   For great is your steadfast love toward me;
      you have delivered my soul from the depths of Sheol.

14   O God, the insolent rise up against me;
      a band of ruffians seeks my life,
      and they do not set you before them.
15   But you, O Lord, are a God merciful and gracious,
      slow to anger and abounding in steadfast love and
      faithfulness.
16   Turn to me and be gracious to me;
      give your strength to your servant;
      save the child of your serving girl.
17   Show me a sign of your favor,
      so that those who hate me may see it and be put to
      shame,
      because you, LORD, have helped me and comforted me.

Commentary

From beginning to end, this psalm is so full of loving trust that we hardly know that the Psalmist is suffering. Not until we come to verse 14, do we discover what the problems are:

O God, the insolent rise up against me;
      a band of ruffians seeks my life,
      and they do not set you before them.

(Ps. 86:14)

Even so, the Psalmist appears calm. The rest of the psalm explains why.

The Psalmist approaches God with specific needs. Each of the first four verses address God in the same form:

- for I am poor and needy (v. 1)
- for I am devoted to you (v. 2)

- for to you do I cry all day (v. 3)
- for to you, O Lord, I lift up my soul (v. 4)

The Psalmist opens his heart to God who is the savior.

In presenting his needs to God, the Psalmist does not wallow in self-pity, but turns from his own pain to God. In particular, the focus is on God as the God of mercy. The Psalmist uses the well-known formula of prayer taken from Exod. 34:6–7:

- God is good and forgiving, abounding in steadfast love (Ps. 86:5).
- God is merciful and gracious, slow to anger and abounding in steadfast love and faithfulness (Ps. 86:15).

Such a well-known formula provides the right words in an emergency. Formulas also carry with them the memory of the times and the spirit in which they have been used. For instance, this particular formula is woven into the prayers for Yom Kippur, the Day of Repentance and Atonement (see Lev. 23:23–32). The memories evoked by such formula prayers have a healing or strengthening effect on those who recall them.

The Psalmist places additional focus on God's mercy by using the four-lettered name of YHWH, translated as "LORD," four times throughout the psalm. This name particularly connotes mercy. In the time of the Second Temple, only the High Priest could recite it out loud and then only on Yom Kippur. Great ceremonies were attached to the pronunciation of the Name. In this psalm, the four-fold pronunciation of the Name proclaims the Psalmist's trust in God's mercy: "There is none like you among the gods, O Lord" (v. 8). The acknowledgment that "You alone are God" (v. 10) empowers the Psalmist to face whatever may come. Whatever happens to the Psalmist happens only out of love and mercy.

The Psalmist wants to be faithful and to walk in truth with an undivided heart. Even though his life is threatened, he begs, "Teach me your way, O LORD" (v. 11). The psalm closes on a note of confidence: "Show me a sign of your favor / . . . because you, LORD, have helped me and comforted me" (v. 17).

Psalm 86 shows us that God will lead and provide for us if we but call on and have confidence in God's mercy. Even when our very life is threatened, we can rejoice in our God, who is like no other.

Reflections

❑ The Psalmist justifies his plea for help by reminding God of his devotion, prayer, and service to God. Examine your own life with these questions: Am I truly devoted to God? Do I pray to God only in times of need? How do I serve God?

❑ In a spirit of loving confidence, identify an area of personal, communal, or societal poverty and need. As in verses 2–4 of Psalm 86, tell God why you need divine help and make a case for why God should help you. Then express your confidence in God's mercy. In short, write your own version of Psalm 86 that follows the same format but expresses your needs, your faith, and your trust.

❑ Where is your heart right now? Pray for the grace of single-heartedness using these words from the psalm: "Give me an undivided heart to revere your name" (v. 11).

❑ The Psalmist is sure of deliverance. He resolves to live a life of faithful obedience. Are there other orientations you need to take in your life? What aspects of your life need conversion? Reflect on them. Then renew your commitment to God's will by repeating, "Teach me your way, O LORD" (v. 11).

❑ Close your meditation by pondering God's merciful gifts to you. After memories of each gifts, pray: "You, Lord, have helped me and comforted me" (v. 17). Resolve to help and comfort someone else.

Memory Verse

There is none like you among the gods, O Lord.

(Ps. 86:8)

How Much Longer, O Lord?

The Psalmist decries the many depredations that have befallen God's servants. The key question he asks God is: How long? How long will God's punishment go on? God's mercy has no limits, nor has God's justice. Knowing this justice gives the Psalmist reason for hope and, in God's time, cause for rejoicing.

Psalm 79

1   O God, the nations have come into your inheritance;
        they have defiled your holy temple;
        they have laid Jerusalem in ruins.
2   They have given the bodies of your servants
        to the birds of the air for food,
        the flesh of your faithful to the wild animals of the
            earth.
3   They have poured out their blood like water
        all around Jerusalem,
        and there was no one to bury them.
4   We have become a taunt to our neighbors,
        mocked and derided by those around us.

5   How long, O Lord? Will you be angry forever?
        Will your jealous wrath burn like fire?
6   Pour out your anger on the nations
        that do not know you,
    And on the kingdoms
        that do not call on your name.
7   For they have devoured Jacob
        and laid waste his habitation.

8 Do not remember against us the iniquities of our
        ancestors;
    let your compassion come speedily to meet us,
        for we are brought very low.
9 Help us, O God of our salvation,
        for the glory of your name;
    deliver us, and forgive our sins,
        for your name's sake.
10 Why should the nations say,
        "Where is their God?"
    Let the avenging of the outpoured blood of your servants
        be known among the nations before our eyes.

11 Let the groans of the prisoners come before you;
        according to your great power preserve those doomed
            to die.
12 Return sevenfold into the bosom of our neighbors
        the taunts with which they taunted you, O Lord!
13 Then we your people, the flock of your pasture,
        will give thanks to you forever;
        from generation to generation we will recount your
            praise.

Commentary

This passionate psalm laments the desecration of the Temple and
the destruction of Jerusalem. The first four verses describe the disaster: the enemy has ravaged Jerusalem, defiled the Temple, and
massacred the people. Now their blood flows through the valleys
surrounding Jerusalem, and their unburied corpses have become
food for birds and animals. In addition, the enemy gloats over
the misfortunes of the people. The Psalmist acknowledges that
God uses the enemy as a tool to punish the disobedient, unfaith-
ful children of Israel.

In the second part of the psalm, the Psalmist screams in
pain: "How long, O LORD? Will you be angry forever? / Will your
jealous wrath burn like fire?" (v. 5). He pleads for forgiveness, especially if the destruction is punishment for the sins of ancestors.

Then, he argues that God should stop the disaster so that other people cannot question God's love for the Israelites.

Despite God's wrath, the Psalmist has not lost hope or trust because the chastised remain God's chosen people, the people to whom God has revealed the divine self. So the Psalmist begs, "Pour out your anger on the nations / that do not know you" (v. 6).

Part of the Psalmist's belief is that when God's people suffer, God also suffers even though, like a good parent, God inflicts the punishment. The destroyers lay waste to God's inheritance, God's Holy Temple, the holy place where God dwells and from which God's word spreads to the nations. When God's servants are given "to the birds of the air for food," it is God's flesh that is given (v. 2). When their blood flows, God's blood flows (v. 3). When God's servants are abused, God is abused.

The early rabbis meditated upon why God appeared to Moses in a lowly thorn bush. They concluded that God appeared in the thorn bush to demonstrate the divine willingness to share in the sufferings of the Hebrew slaves. Just as they were lowly and oppressed, so is God's presence, caught like a bird in the thorns of the bush, a symbol of God's readiness to share the fate of the people.

In verses 8–13, the Psalmist cries to God for mercy and compassion. Even when the chosen people feel afflicted, God leaves a way open for them to talk with God. So they cling to God in their trying circumstances and confess their sins, their pain, their bitter indignation, and their powerlessness to God, trusting that God will understand them and have mercy. Reduced to prayer, which is all that is left to them, they find strength and hope.

If this psalm shocks us with the harshness of God's justice, we should be even more amazed at the psalm's closing verse. Hope and confidence burst through the frightening darkness. Despite what has happened, death and destruction are not the last words. Salvation will come:

> Then we your people, the flock of your pasture,
>> will give thanks to you forever;
>>> from generation to generation we will recount your praise

(Ps. 79:13)

This time has not yet come, but even in the midst of destruction, the Psalmist remembers that the people are still the flock of God's pasture. The memory sows hope in destruction: "We . . . will give thanks to you forever" (v. 13).

Reflections

❑ Our sins often cause pain. Recall an instance when your sin caused pain to both you and others. Call your sin by name. Words give recognition to sin and open the way for repentance. Slowly recite verse 8.

❑ Reflect on the sins of your nation. Name the sin and your role in it, whether it is a sin of commission or omission. Pray over it with verse 9.

❑ The innocent suffer, and suffering is not always caused by personal sins. At such times, we need to proclaim our innocence. Recall a time when you suffered unjustly. Plead your innocence to God. Ask for the grace to let go of your grievance.

❑ God often prevents an enemy from afflicting us or danger from overtaking us. We may never know the number of times someone wanted to harm us and God prevented it. Reflect on the suffering that you have been spared in life. Recite verse 13 in thanksgiving.

❑ Rabbi Levi Yitzchak of Berdichev viewed suffering as a tool for salvation: "When one wishes to transform a small vessel into a large vessel, the small vessel must first be broken. So God, blessed be He, in His desire to see man grow, confronts him with suffering or illness, which represents the breaking of the small vessel" (Pesach Schindler, *Hasidic Responses to the Holocaust in the Light of Hasidic Thought*, p. 35). Recall a time when you were the small vessel that was broken, a time when you have been purified and deepened by suffering. Praise God for this moment.

❑ Prayer may be the only means to alleviate suffering. Pray over a situation of suffering now. Make use of Psalm 79.

Memory Verse

How long, O LORD?

(Ps. 79:5)

How Can We Sing?

This psalm declares that we can hold on to faith and hope even when we lose what is most precious to us and the bottom falls out of our life. In 587 B.C.E. the Babylonians destroyed the sacred city of Jerusalem and dragged its residents off to captivity. Now the captors mock the captives by telling them to sing their Zion songs, cast off their mourning, and be happy in this alien land. The people of Israel refuse to accommodate to the pagan culture. Their joy is the memory of Jerusalem. Their resistance becomes a silent anthem of hope.

Psalm 137

1   By the rivers of Babylon—
            there we sat down and there we wept
            when we remembered Zion.
2   On the willows there
            we hung up our harps.
3   For there our captors
            asked us for songs,
    and our tormentors asked for mirth, saying,
            "Sing us one of the songs of Zion!"

4   How could we sing the LORD's song
            in a foreign land?
5   If I forget you, O Jerusalem,
            let my right hand wither!
6   Let my tongue cling to the roof of my mouth,
            if I do not remember you,
    if I do not set Jerusalem
            above my highest joy.

7   Remember, O LORD, against the Edomites
         the day of Jerusalem's fall,
     how they said, "Tear it down! Tear it down!
         Down to its foundations!"
8   O daughter Babylon, you devastator!
         Happy shall they be who pay you back
         what you have done to us!
9   Happy shall they be who take your little ones
         and dash them against the rock!

Commentary

The lesson of this psalm is how not to forget. If tragedies happen, our joy and means of survival will be the memory of God's faithfulness and our hope in God's mercy, confirmed by our noncompliance and nonaccommodation. Seen in this light, the anger of Psalm 137 serves as a song of hope.

For the people of Israel, Jerusalem is the special dwelling place of God. In the Book of Kings, the Lord told Solomon at the dedication ceremony of the Temple "My eyes and my heart will be there for all time" (1 Kings 9:3).

The rabbis reconciled this text with Prov. 15:3, which says that the eyes of the Lord are in every place, keeping watch on the evil and the good. The rabbis reasoned that God is everywhere, but in order for God to be everywhere, God must definitely be in at least one place. That place is Jerusalem. Through Jerusalem, all other places can become sacred.

Thus, the destruction of Jerusalem and its Temple was an abomination of the highest order because it was the destruction of the place that made all other places holy. Its destruction diminished God's presence in the world. Hence the Psalmist says,

If I forget you, O Jerusalem,
    let my right hand wither!
Let my tongue cling to the roof of my mouth,
    if I do not remember you,
if I do not set Jerusalem
    above my highest joy

(Ps. 137:5–6)

To add abomination to abomination, the captors tell the people to entertain them by singing their holy songs, the ones they sang before God in the Temple. The people of Israel reply, "How could we sing the LORD's song / in a foreign land?" (v. 4).

Life would be infinitely easier for the captives if they would just give in and adopt Babylonian ways. But by refusing, they hold fast to their identity as a people of God. Fidelity to God is sometimes reduced to not forgetting, not making peace with the enemy, not accommodating to the ungodly lifestyle.

In keeping with the honesty and passion of the Psalms, the Psalmist invokes God's wrath upon the enemy and adds,

> Happy shall they be who pay you back
> what you have done to us!
> Happy shall they be who take your little ones
> and dash them against the rock!
>
> (Ps. 137:8-9)

This is the language of nonaccommodation and nonadaptation. The exiles from Israel left the punishment of Babylon to God, but the vehemence of the language indicates their noncompliance with Babylon and their link with Jerusalem.

King Cyrus of Persia defeated Babylon and decreed that the exiles could return (Ezra 1:1–4). This vindicated the faith of the Jews, and a new period of Jewish history began under the leadership of Ezra, Nehemiah, and other community leaders.

Reflections

❑ God chose a special people, the Jews, to whom to make the divine self known. God also chose a special place, Jerusalem, so that all other places could be recognized as holy. Pray verses 5 and 6 several times.

What is a sacred site for you, a place where the presence of God is strong for you? Sit quietly and bring this place to mind. If possible, go there. Whether in your memory or at the holy site, offer a prayer or song of thanks for this place.

❑ Recall a situation in which you have felt or feel bereft: a broken relationship, an injustice done to you, a betrayal by someone, a separation from your home or a special place, a violation committed against you. What sacred memories helped you hold on, keep living, and sustain hope? Thank God for these sacred memories.

If you are in a situation of injustice or oppression now, how can you sustain your hope by not accommodating, by peacefully resisting? Ask God for the graces you need to keep your hope alive.

❑ Write your own version of Psalm 137. Do not be afraid of anger and bitterness. God knows what is in your heart; letting it out helps you to claim it. Turn the anger to positive energy in order to get past the suffering.

❑ Meditate on these lines from Emily Dickinson's poem about the paradoxical value of despair:

> I cannot live with You—
> It would be Life—
> And Life is over there—
> Behind the Shelf
>
> The Sexton keeps the Key to—
> Putting up
> Our Life—His Porcelain—
> Like a Cup—
>
> . . . . .
> So We must meet apart—
> You there—I—here—
> With just the Door ajar
> That Oceans are—and Prayer—
> And that White Sustenance—
> Despair—

(Sculley Bradley et al., eds.,
The American Tradition in Literature, J. 640)

When our souls are in exile from our true self, from people we love, or from a special place, how is despair a "white sustenance" like prayer? Can you rejoice in your despair?

❑ Sing one of your sacred songs or listen to music that speaks to you of the God of life. Let the music remind you of the sacredness of yourself, God's work of art.

Memory Verse

If I forget you, O Jerusalem,
   let my right hand wither!

(Ps. 137:5)

God Leads Us to Repentance

When we sin, ignore God's commands, or destroy our right relationships with God, people, and the earth, the result is chaos in both the self and in creation. Repentance begins to restore the balance. This psalm was composed in response to the grievous sin committed by David and the outpourings of his contrite heart (2 Samuel 12). The "I" of the psalm can stand for both the individual and the nation.

Psalm 51

1 Have mercy on me, O God,
   according to your steadfast love;
  according to your abundant mercy
   blot out my transgressions.
2 Wash me thoroughly from my iniquity,
   and cleanse me from my sin.

3 For I know my transgressions,
   and my sin is ever before me.
4 Against you, you alone, have I sinned,
   and done what is evil in your sight,
  so that you are justified in your sentence
   and blameless when you pass judgment.
5 Indeed, I was born guilty,
   a sinner when my mother conceived me.

6 You desire truth in the inward being;
   therefore teach me wisdom in my secret heart.
7 Purge me with hyssop, and I shall be clean;
   wash me, and I shall be whiter than snow.

8	Let me hear joy and gladness;
	let the bones that you have crushed rejoice.
9	Hide your face from my sins,
	and blot out all my iniquities.

10	Create in me a clean heart, O God,
	and put a new and right spirit within me.
11	Do not cast me away from your presence,
	and do not take your holy spirit from me.
12	Restore to me the joy of your salvation,
	and sustain in me a willing spirit.

13	Then I will teach transgressors your ways,
	and sinners will return to you.
14	Deliver me from bloodshed, O God,
	O God of my salvation,
	and my tongue will sing aloud of your deliverance.

15	O Lord, open my lips,
	and my mouth will declare your praise.
16	For you have no delight in sacrifice;
	if I were to give a burnt offering, you would not be pleased.
17	The sacrifice acceptable to God is a broken spirit;
	a broken and contrite heart, O God, you will not despise.

18	Do good to Zion in your good pleasure;
	rebuild the walls of Jerusalem,
19	then you will delight in right sacrifices,
	in burnt offerings and whole burnt offerings;
	then bulls will be offered on your altar.

Commentary

God created within us two temples in which God resides. From the temple of our heart proceed love, mercy, compassion, sympathy, and joy. With the temple of the mind, we seek to know God. Therefore, we can never leave the divine presence even if we sin and defile the divine abode "which remains with [us] in

the midst of [our] uncleannesses" (Lev. 16:16). However, our infinite hunger for the divine often wars with our lust, greed, envy, hatred, and selfishness.

Sin causes suffering and a sense of loss. The sinner becomes enslaved and defiled; the innermost sanctuary is sullied. Blinded by sin, the sinner no longer feels God's presence. Even so, God resides within. The profound mourning experienced by the sinner is a prerequisite for repentance. The divine presence prompts this mourning.

Sin is a spiritual illness that leads to the disintegration of the whole personality. As with physical disease, such illness may be ignored or denied because of fear. But the longer the denial lasts, the worse the sickness becomes. If the sinner enters the mourning that accompanies sin, the first element of recovery is at hand: that is, acknowledgment of the sin or a recognition that "I have sinned."

Deep regret, longing for purification and cleansing, and a plea for God's forgiveness form the second element in repentance. The third element is the determination not to sin again, and the fourth is forgiveness and new life. All of these elements of repentance are contained in Psalm 51.

1. Element one involves recognition and confession of sins:
- "For I know my transgressions" (v. 3)
- I have "done what is evil in your sight" (v. 4).
- "I was born guilty, / a sinner when my mother conceived me" (v. 5).

The Psalmist does not blame his parents or corruption by original sin for his guilt. Rather, he asserts his own experience of finitude—that limitation and guilt beset him from the beginning of his life to the present.

2. Element two involves asking God for forgiveness:
- "Have mercy on me" (v. 1).
- "Wash me thoroughly from my iniquity" (v. 2).
- "Cleanse me from my sin" (v. 2).

3. Element three includes the determination not to sin again:
- "Create in me a clean heart" (v. 10).
- "Put a new and right spirit within me" (v. 10).
- "Sustain in me a willing spirit" (v. 12).

4. Element four consists of forgiveness and new life:

- "A broken and contrite heart, O God, you will not despise" (v. 17).
- "Restore to me the joy of your salvation" (v. 12).
- "My tongue will sing aloud of your deliverance" (v. 14).
- "My mouth will declare your praise" (v. 15).

Joy accompanies repentance. Cleansed and purified, the sinner is allowed back into the presence of God. To repent means to return, to turn around, to turn toward God. The return of even one sinner creates more joy in heaven than ninety-nine others who need not repent.

If on the one hand sin is blotted out, on the other hand it is always "before me" because, through sin and repentance, our relationship with God is deepened. When we have lost something precious we treasure it all the more when it is found. In our relationship with God, the joy in reunion outstrips any joy we had before we sinned.

Repentance is a great gift. In repentance, we gradually come to know God and dwell continually in the divine presence. We should take repentance with us because of our constant tendency to wander away from God. Through it, we will keep our faces turned toward God, who will let the divine face shine upon us in a way we cannot doubt: "A broken and contrite heart, O God, you will not despise" (v. 17). God's forgiveness turns our mourning into joy, so our "mouth will declare [God's] praise" (v. 15).

Reflections

❑ Examine your conscience. First repeat this prayer from the psalm: "You desire truth in the inward being; / therefore teach me wisdom in my secret heart" (v. 6). Listen as you pray, especially to any signs of mourning that lurk in your heart. God will speak.

When you are ready, these questions may aid your examination: Do I exploit others? Do I take people for granted? Do I pollute nature and neglect the environment? Do I abuse my body? Do I use my gifts for love and justice?

❏ Sometimes loneliness results from the alienation sin causes. Repentance means returning or turning around to God, to other people, and away from sin. Repentance dispels loneliness. Examine any recent instances of your alienation from God, from another person, or from nature. Use the steps of repentance to return to and heal these relationships.

❏ Our inclination toward doing good clashes with our pull toward doing evil. This tension generates creative energy; the conflict enriches our character. Ponder how the tension between these two inclinations within you has challenged, deepened, and enriched you.

❏ Ponder your sins, and then pray a litany asking forgiveness. Name the sin, then pray: "Have mercy on me; cleanse me from my sin."

❏ Select two of your most persistent sins and, while praying "sustain in me a willing spirit," determine practical ways you can cooperate with God's grace to cease sinning in each way.

❏ Rejoice in God's gifts of repentance and forgiveness. Sing a hymn of joy like "Amazing Grace." Quietly chant the words: "My mouth will declare your praise." Tell a trusted friend about God's goodness towards you.

❏ Suffering can uplift, cleanse, purify, ennoble, and expand the soul. Ponder some of the sufferings around you from this point of view. Keep looking until you find light.

❏ Unconditional and total surrender to God frees us from all other enslavements and bondages. Pray sections of this psalm as a renewed dedication and surrender of yourself to God.

❏ "Do you not know that you are God's temple?" (1 Cor. 3:16). Enter into this interior temple and speak to your divine guest. Ask that you may be built up into a worthy dwelling place of the Lord.

Memory Verse

O Lord open my lips,
and my mouth will declare your praise.

(Ps. 51:15)

Seasoned Joy:
Psalms of Experience

Let everything that breathes praise the LORD!

(Ps. 150:6)

The psalms in this part of the book are called the psalms of experience because the speaker, having lived a full life, knows that God is a God of steadfast love. Those who have arrived at this point are God-oriented, mature, and grounded. They are not easily disturbed, depressed, or discouraged. They are not bitter and do not project blame unto others. They have suffered and seen the pain of other people, so they show deep compassion. Praise of God comes to them naturally, spontaneously, and often. These are the people Jesus addressed when he said: "'Peace I leave with you; my peace I give unto you. I do not give to you as the world gives. Do not let your hearts be troubled, and do not let them be afraid'" (John 14:27).

Meditation 11, on Psalm 27, expresses supreme joy, deep peace, and absence of fear. Meditation 12, on Psalm 139, is an intimate love song between the speaker and God. Meditation 13, on Psalm 96, expresses rapturous joy because God is sovereign. Meditation 14, on Psalm 103, is one of the most joyful psalms in the whole Psalter because of the conviction that God is a God of steadfast love. Meditation 15, on Psalm 150, is a grand symphony of praise where the whole of creation does what it was made to do, namely: Praise the Lord, alleluia!

Rejoice!
God, My Light and Salvation

Psalm 27 proclaims the strong faith and sure confidence that come from a direct experience of God. The Psalmist has conquered his last enemy: fear. Not even death or the companions of death—sickness, aging, and failure—frighten him any more. Meditating on this psalm can help take the sting out of death.

Psalm 27

1   The LORD is my light and my salvation;
        whom shall I fear?
    The LORD is the stronghold of my life;
        of whom shall I be afraid?

2   When evildoers assail me
        to devour my flesh—
    my adversaries and foes—
        they shall stumble and fall.

3   Though an army encamp against me,
        my heart shall not fear;
    though war rise up against me,
        yet I will be confident.

4   One thing I asked of the LORD,
        that I will seek after;
    to live in the house of the LORD,
        all the days of my life,
    to behold the beauty of the LORD,
        and to inquire in his temple.

5   For he will hide me in his shelter
        in the day of trouble;
    he will conceal me under the cover of his tent;
        he will set me high on a rock.

6   Now my head is lifted up
        above my enemies all around me,
    and I will offer in his tent
        sacrifices with shouts of joy;
    I will sing and make melody to the LORD.

7   Hear, O LORD, when I cry aloud,
        be gracious to me and answer me!
8   "Come," my heart says, "seek his face!"
        Your face, LORD, do I seek.
9   Do not hide your face from me.

    Do not turn your servant away in anger,
        you who have been my help.
    Do not cast me off, do not forsake me,
        O God of my salvation!
10 If my father and mother forsake me,
        the LORD will take me up.

11 Teach me your way, O LORD,
        and lead me on a level path
        because of my enemies.
12 Do not give me up to the will of my adversaries,
        for false witnesses have risen against me,
        and they are breathing out violence.

13 I believe that I shall see the goodness of the LORD
        in the land of the living.
14 Wait for the LORD;
        be strong, and let your heart take courage;
        wait for the LORD!

Commentary

Nothing that happens can shake the Psalmist's confidence in
God. Verses 1–3 express joy and confidence in the Lord. The first

verse declares that God is the Psalmist's light, salvation, and stronghold, so "of whom shall I be afraid?" Not even death is frightening.

Verses 4–6 describe the basic longing of the Psalmist's heart: to know God, to contemplate God, and to dwell continually in God's presence in the house of the Lord. Only God can satisfy the thirst of a soul. Only God can calm restless strife, life's anguish, and the fear of annihilation. The Psalmist is armed with, and clothed in, the divine presence. God is his shelter, his tent, his rock.

The third section of the psalm, verses 7–12, is different in tone from the other two sections. Keenly aware of human frailty, the Psalmist begs God: do not hide your face from me; do not put your servant away in your anger; do not cast me off; do not forsake me. The inspiration for this pleading comes from the still small voice in his heart: "'Come,' my heart says, 'seek his face!'" (v. 8). The Psalmist is obedient—he does not simply beg, but puts forth reasons why God should listen: I seek your face (v. 8); in the past you have been my help (v. 9) ; those who slander me have risen up against me (v. 12).

Verse 13 can be translated: "I would have despaired unless I had believed that I would see the goodness of the Lord in the land of the living." Thus, the last verse of the psalm cautions: wait for the Lord. The Lord will answer. How does the Psalmist know this? Because of the Lord's name. The psalm opened with a double invocation of the Name, and the psalm closes with the pronunciation of the Name. All is enclosed within God. Hence wait, be strong, take courage, wait.

As to fear of death, the speaker is convinced that God is with us. We are not alone.

- Do not worry about the future—God abides with us now. Here in the present is light, protection, and shelter.
- Plead and reason with God. Ask for what you need.
- Express confidence in God's merciful presence.
- Live in the presence of God. Learn God's ways. Remembering God empowers us.
- Wait patiently. God is faithful and will not abandon us.

Reflections

❑ For the Psalmist, God is light, salvation, and stronghold. Choose three meaningful nouns that describe God for you: The Lord is . . . Conclude the sentence by asking: "Whom shall I fear?"

 Now list people, situations, or challenges that threaten, slander, frighten, or cause you to suffer in any way. These enemies can be personal enemies or enemies of humanity. After each one write: "Of whom shall I be afraid?"

❑ Pray repeatedly verses 4–6. Ponder their meaning for you. Is living in the house of God all that you seek? Do you make offerings to God and sing to the Lord? Dialog with God about your relationship.

❑ Is there some situation in which you feel the need for God's presence? Some area of your life where God does not abide with you? Bring this situation to mind, and pray for God's presence, recalling the words of the Scriptures: "'When you search for me, you will find me; if you seek me with all your heart, I will let you find me'" (Jer. 29:13–14).

❑ Those who recognize God's presence already dwell in the house of Lord. List all of the places and people who today help you behold the beauty of the Lord. Give thanks for them. Try to express your gratitude for their presence in some tangible way.

❑ Say Psalm 27 every day for a week as a closing night prayer.

❑ In Leo Tolstoy's story "The Death of Ivan Ilych," Ivan dies a horrible death. When Ivan learns that he is dying of cancer, he begins to struggle with the emptiness of his past. Early in the story, Tolstoy gives a hint as to why the death is so painful: "Ivan Ilych's life had been most simple and most ordinary and therefore most terrible" (Leo Tolstoy, *The Raid and Other Stories*, p. 235). As his dying proceeds irrevocably, the nature of his torture becomes apparent.

It was true, as the doctor said, that Ivan Ilych's physical sufferings were terrible, but worse than the physical sufferings were his mental sufferings which were his chief torture.

His mental sufferings were due to the fact that that night, as he looked at [his servant's] sleepy, good-natured face with its prominent cheek-bones, the question suddenly occurred to him: "What if my whole life has really been wrong?" (Tolstoy, *The Raid and Other Stories*, p. 276)

Tolstoy concludes that Ivan's life had, indeed, been all wrong: he had never really loved, he had been so busy avoiding conflict that he had never formed any convictions, and he had conformed even in the smallest customs so that he would be accepted by all the other boring men like himself.

Reflect on this question of Ivan's: "'What if my whole life has really been wrong?'" What does Psalm 27 suggest about making life right? Apply it to your unique life story. Talk with God about it.

Ask yourself: "If I had only a year to live, how would I want to live that time?"

❑ Offer your concerns about death to God. When you feel anxious, pray: "Take courage, wait for the Lord!"

Memory Verse

Your face, LORD, do I seek.

(Ps. 27:8)

Rejoice!
God Is Present

Psalm 139, a psalm of rejoicing, comes from the Psalmist's intimate personal experience of God. The Psalmist's language reflects this intimacy. In the psalm, God is pictured as a judge, a guide, a weaver, and a midwife. Above all, God is a friend and a lover. The intimacy of the psalm invites us to an openness with God that we may not be used to.

Psalm 139

1   O LORD, you have searched me and known me.
2   You know when I sit down and when I rise up;
        you discern my thoughts from far away.
3   You search out my path and my lying down,
        and are acquainted with all my ways.
4   Even before a word is on my tongue,
        O LORD, you know it completely.
5   You hem me in, behind and before,
        and lay your hand upon me.
6   Such knowledge is too wonderful for me;
        it is so high that I cannot attain it.

7   Where can I go from your spirit?
        Or where can I flee from your presence?
8   If I ascend to heaven, you are there;
        if I make my bed in Sheol, you are there.
9   If I take the wings of the morning
        and settle at the farthest limits of the sea,
10 even there your hand shall lead me,
        and your right hand shall hold me fast.

11 If I say, "Surely the darkness shall cover me,
        and the light around me become night,"
12 even the darkness is not dark to you;
        the night is as bright as the day,
        for darkness is as light to you.

13 For it was you who formed my inward parts;
        you knit me together in my mother's womb.
14 I praise you, for I am fearfully and wonderfully made.
        Wonderful are your works;
    that I know very well.
15   My frame was not hidden from you,
    when I was being made in secret,
        intricately woven in the depths of the earth.
16 Your eyes beheld my unformed substance.
        In your book were written
        all the days that were formed for me,
        when none of them as yet existed.
17 How weighty to me are your thoughts, O God!
        How vast is the sum of them!
18 I try to count them—they are more than the sand;
        I come to the end—I am still with you.

19 O that you would kill the wicked, O God,
        and that the bloodthirsty would depart from me—
20 those who speak of you maliciously,
        and lift themselves up against you for evil!
21 Do I not hate those who hate you, O LORD?
        And do I not loathe those who rise up against you?
22 I hate them with perfect hatred;
        I count them as my enemies.
23 Search me, O God, and know my heart;
        test me and know my thoughts.
24 See if there is any wicked way in me,
        and lead me in the way everlasting.

Commentary

Psalm 139 is one of the most intimate and personal psalms in the
Bible. Throughout it, the Psalmist addresses God as "you" rather

than in the third person. The psalm opens in verses 1–6 by invoking God's most personal and tender name, though this is not evident in the translation of "Lord" from the Hebrew. The Psalmist declares in effect: "Lord, you know me in a way no one else does. You know how I feel, how I think, what I do, where I am going, what my next move will be. You know what I am going to say even before I say it. You know me more intimately than a woman knows her husband, than a mother knows her child. Your hands enfold me as my shelter and set my safe boundaries." In short, "such knowledge is too wonderful for me; too high that I cannot attain it."

In the second section (vv. 7–12), the Psalmist acknowledges that because of God's presence to each person, God knows the person intimately. No place exists where God is not. Through a series of hypothetical questions and imaginary trips, the Psalmist ponders: "If I go up to heaven like Elijah (2 Kings 2:9–10), you are there. If I descend to the depths of Sheol like Korah and Dathan (Num. 16:29–33), you are there. If I fly to the remotest east where the dawn rises or the distant west, where the sun sinks into the sea, you are there. If I fly with the speed of the winged dawn, I cannot escape you. Everywhere, your hand is upon me, leading me and holding me. Not even darkness can hide me for darkness is as light to you."

God's omniscience and God's omnipresence make God's intimate involvement in our life obvious. Each of us is individually and carefully formed by the hands of God. Every faculty and every sense have been chosen and lovingly bestowed. Thus, in the third section, the Psalmist addresses God, the weaver: You formed all my parts. You knit me together in my mother's womb, molded me into form, caressed me with your look into pulsating life. O, but I am wonderfully and fearfully made (vv. 13–18). Our thirsts, inclinations, potencies are all gifts that lead to wonder

How weighty to me are your thoughts, O God!
How vast is the sum of them!
I try to count them—they are more than the sand;
I come to the end—I am still with you"

(Ps. 139:17–18)

71

The last verses, 19–24, are a plea to see divine justice at work and to remain faithful. The psalm began by saying, "O LORD, you have searched me and known me," now it closes with, "search me, O God, and know my heart." We pray that God will bring to light our true self and lead us to it.

Reflections

❏ One of the first steps in intimacy with God is that of repentance and purification: Who shall stand in the presence of God?

> Those who have clean hands and pure hearts,
> > who do not lift up their souls to what is false,
> > and do not swear deceitfully.

> (Ps. 24:4)

Pray for radical self-honesty by reciting this verse several times:

> Create in me a clean heart, O God,
> > and put a new and right spirit within me.

> (Ps. 51:10)

Then pray Psalm 139, lingering over lines that seem to have special importance for you.

❏ Ponder again verses 1–6, which address God personally as "you." God willingly enters into a mutual relationship with us that allows us to stand up and be counted as one of the wonders of God's creation. Talk to God as "you," telling of your gratitude for the many gifts you have been given.

❏ Thank God for the way God made you. Ask that you may develop your gifts and talents according to the divine will. Let the following verses from the psalm play as background music during this exercise:

> For it was you who formed my inward parts;
> > you knit me together in my mother's womb.
> I praise you, for I am fearfully and wonderfully made.

> (vv. 13–14)

❏ Many of us have been taught to devalue our body and our gifts of personality (humor, kindness, ability to listen, and so on). Compose a litany of thanks to God for parts of your body and for these gifts of personality. Pray the litany, ending each phrase: "I praise you, for I am fearfully and wonderfully made." For example: "For my hands with which I caress and serve my loved ones, I praise you, for I am fearfully and wonderfully made." Or, "for dancing, a way to express my joy and body-self, I praise you, for I am fearfully and wonderfully made."

❏ Ponder verses 13–18 and the image of God working and dwelling within you, helping you to be creative at whatever age you are. What new thing is God inviting you to bring into being? What problem needs solving that will make life better for the human family? What creative solutions—even small ones—can you bring to the problem? The weaver God stirs within us, urging us to create; call on the weaver God to stir you to action.

❏ With a heart grateful and awed by God's love, pray the following ancient Jewish prayer:

> My God, the soul which you placed within me is pure. You created it; you formed it; you breathed it into me. You preserve it within me; you will take it from me, and restore it to me in the hereafter. So long as the soul is within me, I offer thanks before you, Lord my God and God of my ancestors, maker of all creatures, Lord of all souls. Blessed art you, O Lord, who restores the souls to the dead. (Adapted from Philip Birnbaum, trans., *Daily Prayer Book*, p. 16)

As you pray this prayer, think of each gift and characteristic you have and see these gifts as lovingly and thoughtfully bestowed upon you.

❏ Seek out someone who needs encouragement to see his or her gifts and power. Do what you can to help restore some dignity to that person.

❏ Rewrite verses 7–12, using categories that apply to your life. For example, "If I ascend the corporate ladder, you are there; if I walk to work, you are there. If I fail in this undertaking, you are there; if I raise my head to the light, you are there."

Memory Verse

I praise you, for I am fearfully and wonderfully made.

(Ps. 139:14)

Rejoice!
God Reigns

The diverse images of God in the Bible help us to understand the many facets of the great mystery of God. Psalm 96 joyously proclaims that God is king. Let us understand the meaning of God as king, and then proclaim with all our heart, "'The LORD is King!'"

Psalm 96

1   O sing to the LORD a new song;
        sing to the LORD, all the earth.

2   Sing to the LORD, bless his name;
        tell of his salvation from day to day.

3   Declare his glory among the nations,
        his marvelous works among all the peoples.

4   For great is the LORD, and greatly to be praised;
        he is to be revered above all gods.

5   For all the gods of the peoples are idols,
        but the LORD made the heavens.

6   Honor and majesty are before him;
        strength and beauty are in his sanctuary.

7   Ascribe to the LORD, O families of the peoples,
        ascribe to the LORD glory and strength.

8   Ascribe to the LORD the glory due his name;
        bring an offering, and come into his courts.

9   Worship the LORD in holy splendor;
        tremble before him, all the earth.

10   Say among the nations, "The LORD is king!
        The world is firmly established; it shall never be moved
        He will judge the peoples with equity."

11   Let the heavens be glad, and let the earth rejoice;
         let the sea roar, and all that fills it;
12   let the field exult, and everything in it.
     Then shall all the trees of the forest sing for joy
13   before the LORD; for he is coming,
         for he is coming to judge the earth.
     He will judge the world with righteousness,
         and the peoples with his truth.

Commentary

In Psalm 96, the Psalmist encourages us to proclaim, "'The LORD is King!'" Recognition of God's kingship frees us from the power of lesser gods and lesser kings. Our ruler must be God alone. Freed from the tyranny of idols, we can rejoice in the true God.

In verses 1–3 of Psalm 96, the Psalmist calls Israel to sing a new song and acknowledge God's sovereignty in a burst of six imperatives:

- sing
- sing
- sing
- bless
- tell
- declare

Verses 4–6 list the reasons for the call. The King is:

- great
- worthy of praise
- supreme over all other gods
- Creator
- filled with honor and majesty, strength and beauty

In verses 7–10, all the nations are invited to join in the jubilation, and are then given directions on how to recognize God's kingship.

- ascribe glory
- bring offerings
- come
- worship
- tremble

Why? Because "'The LORD is King!'" (v. 10).

In verses 11–13, the entire cosmos—heavens, earth, sea, land, trees—is summoned to praise and acknowledge God as king. The king is coming to judge with righteousness and truth.

Narrowly understood, the word "king" may evoke images of oppression, domination, and patriarchal superiority. However, other images in the Torah broaden any narrow image we may have of God as king. Among the first pages of the Bible, God is portrayed as a mother bird, *Ruah*, spirit, hovering over primordial chaos and warming it into life (Gen. 1:2). In the Book of Exodus, God is an eagle in flight, carrying the enslaved on her strong wings to freedom (Exod. 19:4). In Psalm 131 God nurses her child at her breast.

These images refer to the same God who is also king. God is basically incomprehensible, and so we give God many names drawn from analogy. Each of these names, although inadequate, opens up a new facet of our understanding of God. The names we give to God are necessarily drawn from our experience and in our effort to name God, we attribute many names.

We describe God with natural attributes: God is spirit, changeless, all-powerful, all-knowing, eternal. We attribute moral attributes to God: God is holy, righteous, truthful, wise. We use nouns from the professions: God is shepherd, teacher, midwife, physician. We draw images from political life: God is king, warrior, judge. We even draw analogies from the animal world: God is roaring lion, soaring eagle, protective hen, angry mother bear. We use nature: God is light, rock, water, fire, cloud. We do what we can as humans; we need images to relate to God.

We proclaim God's kingship because God is not only tender, loving, and merciful, but also strong, powerful, and ultimately victorious. Thus, the image of God as king has been a favorite image for both Jews and Christians. The Jewish community inaugurates each Sabbath day by reciting Psalms 95–99 and Psalm 27, the kingship psalms. These six psalms stand for the six days of the week and are an acknowledgment that God is king over every day. On Rosh Hashanah, the Jewish New Year, God is enthroned as king. The cantor sings several times in ever-ascending crescendos, "God is King." The *Aleinu* prayer that ends each of the three daily prayer services closes with the affirmation, "The Lord will be King over all the world." Each Jew is encouraged to

recite at least one hundred blessings a day, beginning each one with the formula, "Blessed art thou, Lord our God, King of the universe, for . . ."

The notion of God's kingship is no less important to Christianity. The psalms of God's kingship are recited daily in the church. The Gospels are filled with references to the Kingdom of God. The central prayer of the church is a plea, "Thy kingdom come." When God reigns over all the earth, then all people may be joined in rejoicing.

Reflections

❏ Slowly reread Psalm 96. Linger over the lines and images, especially those that praise God's power. How does God use the divine power? Does God's power reassure you? Talk with God the king about this.

❏ Recite the Lord's Prayer and focus on "thy Kingdom come." What will the Kingdom of God be like? How will God's Reign be different from life as it is today? How are you helping to build the Reign of God? Pray for the graces you need to co-create this reign with God the king.

❏ Verse 5 says, "for all the gods of the peoples are idols." Glance through newspapers or magazines and try to pick out the "gods of the peoples." Do we put other "kings" above God? Do you? Name any idols that you have. How can you turn from them and proclaim that God alone is your king? Ask God to help you.

❏ If possible, go outside amid glad nature. Marvel at the extravagance and exuberance of a kingly God who could make such exotic, abundant creations. Pray verses 11-13; sing a hymn of thanksgiving. Consider adding a movement to your prayer called "shuckling." Lift up your hands in praise or fold your arms across your heart in an embrace, sway from side to side or back and forth in time with your singing: put your body into the song.

❑ With the Reign of God, justice will be restored to the earth and then all of nature will join in singing. Do something today to help nature sing. Plant flowers or vegetables, pick up garbage, recycle papers. Rejoice in concert with nature.

Memory Verse

"The LORD is King!"

(Ps. 96:10)

Rejoice!
God Is Steadfast Love

Psalm 103 is a psalm of arrival for us. We have moved from the psalms of innocence through the psalms of protest and now to the psalms of experience. We have examined God's ways, and we rejoice. Whether or not we understand these ways, God *is* steadfast love upon whom we can count. In the face of contradictions, even in the face of evil, we will bless God.

Psalm 103

1   Bless the LORD, O my soul,
          and all that is within me,
          bless his holy name.
2   Bless the LORD, O my soul,
          and do not forget all his benefits—
3   who forgives all your iniquity,
          who heals all your diseases,
4   who redeems your life from the Pit,
          who crowns you with steadfast love and mercy,
5   who satisfies you with good as long as you live
          so that your youth is renewed like the eagle's.

6   The LORD works vindication
          and justice for all who are oppressed.
7   He made known his ways to Moses,
          his acts to the people of Israel.
8   The LORD is merciful and gracious,
          slow to anger and abounding in steadfast love.
9   He will not always accuse,
          nor will he keep his anger forever.

10   He does not deal with us according to our sins,
         nor repay us according to our iniquities.

11   For as the heavens are high above the earth,
         so great is his steadfast love toward those who fear
            him;

12   as far as the east is from the west,
         so far he removes our transgressions from us.

13   As a father has compassion for his children,
         so the LORD has compassion for those who fear him.

14   For he knows how we were made;
         he remembers that we are dust.

15   As for mortals, their days are like grass;
         they flourish like a flower of the field;

16   for the wind passes over it, and it is gone,
         and its place knows it no more.

17   But the steadfast love of the LORD is from everlasting to
         everlasting
         on those who fear him,
         and his righteousness to children's children,

18   to those who keep his covenant
         and remember to do his commandments.

19   The LORD has established his throne in the heavens,
         and his kingdom rules over all.

20   Bless the LORD, O you his angels,
         you mighty ones who do his bidding,
         obedient to his spoken word.

21   Bless the LORD, all his hosts,
         his ministers that do his will.

22   Bless the LORD, all his works,
         in all places of his dominion.
     Bless the LORD, O my soul.

Commentary

Even if we do not understand God's ways, even if we do not understand why tragedy must happen in the world, or why pain or

sorrow afflict us, we do have the key for living with the contradiction that God is a God of steadfast love. Four times in this psalm, the Psalmist reiterates that phrase:

- who crowns you with steadfast love (v. 4)
- abounding in steadfast love (v. 8)
- great is his steadfast love (v. 11)
- the steadfast love of the LORD is from everlasting to everlasting (v. 17)

We can be so sure of this love that we refer to the history of Moses as proof (v. 7). Moses' name evokes God's faithful love in the deliverance of the people from slavery to freedom. The Exodus was fraught with rebellion, hunger, and doubts, but God remained faithful. In the end, the story was summed up in God's words to Moses on the mountain: "'You have seen . . . how I bore you on eagles' wings and brought you to myself'" (Exod. 19:4).

Ancient people believed that the eagle lived to a great age, even one hundred years. The image of the eagle in this psalm expresses our belief in the way God will protect us, even in old age: "who satisfies you with good as long as you live / so that your youth is renewed like the eagle's" (v. 5).

The psalm opens and closes with the one summons the soul must always hear and obey:

Bless the LORD, O my soul,
and all that is within me,
bless his holy name.

(Ps. 103:1)

How can we remember to do this? "Do not forget all his benefits" (v. 2). Benefits are all the rewards, all the good things that we have received in life. The verbs sum up what the benefits are: God is the one who forgives, heals, redeems, and crowns us (vv. 3–5). Moreover, God gives these benefits to everyone: "The LORD works vindication / and justice for all who are oppressed" (v. 6).

Then the Psalmist reminds us that God gives these benefits because it is God's nature to do so:

The LORD is merciful and gracious,
  slow to anger and abounding in steadfast love.

(v. 8)

God's mercy shatters all our expectations. God "does not deal with us according to our sins, / nor repay us according to our iniquities" but "removes our transgressions from us" (vv. 10, 12).

As the Creator, God knows how we are made from the earth, the humus (Genesis 2:7). We are mortal creatures, destined to return to the dust. Instead of leaving us to our fate, God shows pity and acts mercifully toward us.

When we ponder God's steadfast love—all the benefits, forgiveness, and graciousness—the only fitting response is joyful blessing of God's name through singing, praying, and doing God's bidding. Hence, in the last four verses, the Psalmist summons us to bless God. We call on all creation, the angels, the hosts of heaven, God's works, and ourself to bless God.

However, when we pray the psalm we primarily tell ourself, "Bless the Lord, O *my* soul." No matter what other people do or how they feel about God, I will praise the Lord. All that is within me will bless God's holy name.

Reflections

❏ Pray slowly and repeatedly: "Bless the Lord, O my soul . . . all that is within me, bless God's holy name."

Recall the many benefits or gifts that God has given you. As you think of each benefit, pray "Bless the Lord, O my soul. . . . Do not forget all the benefits God has given you."

❏ God "forgives all your iniquity, . . . heals all your diseases" and renews your youth. Taking this as God's word, pray for forgiveness for your iniquities; ask God to heal you from whatever diseases of body or spirit you have; and beseech God to renew you. Address God directly, knowing that God hears you and responds.

❑ Ponder some of the injustices and oppression that regularly make news. Consider some of the injustices and oppressions in your own life. As you recall each instance, pray these lines of the psalm: "The Lord works vindication and justice for all who are oppressed." Then look for ways that people are being called to be God's hands and voice. Thank God for the voices speaking out for justice and mercy.

❑ Pray for peace in your own life, in your community, and in the world. In each instance where peace is needed, ask God for peace and pray: You, God, are "abounding in steadfast love."

❑ To remind yourself of God's steadfast love in your life, remember one or two events that at the time seemed disastrous for you but turned out to be positive moments in your story when you reflected upon them later. Dialog with God about these events, and thank God for being steadfast love.

❑ Write out a prayer, using the format of verses 20–22:
　　Bless the Lord . . .
　　Bless the Lord . . .
　　Bless the Lord . . .
　　Bless the Lord, O my soul.

Memory Verse

Bless the LORD, O my soul.

(Ps. 103:1)

Rejoice!
Be Happy

This book of meditations began with Psalm 1, which teaches us that if we meditate on God's word day and night, we will find happiness. We see that even in sorrow, suffering, and toil, God's steadfast love gives us reason to rejoice. All of reality is called upon to help us to understand and come closer to God: a mother bird, a ruling king, a nursing mother, a rock, the stars, the depths. Now, in Psalm 150, the last psalm, they are called forth again to be part of a great symphony of praise to God.

Psalm 150

1   Praise the LORD!
    Praise God in his sanctuary;
        praise him in his mighty firmament!
2   Praise him for his mighty deeds;
        praise him according to his surpassing greatness!

3   Praise him with trumpet sound;
        praise him with lute and harp!
4   Praise him with tambourine and dance;
        praise him with strings and pipe!
5   Praise him with clanging cymbals;
        praise him with loud clashing cymbals!
6   Let everything that breathes praise the LORD!
    Praise the LORD!

Commentary

Psalm 1 proclaims the importance of God's word in our life. Psalm 150 shows the outcome of a life lived under God's word. Psalm 1 gives the recipe for happiness. Psalm 150 is the result—unrestrained praise.

The title of Psalm 150 is "Praise the LORD" or "Alleluia." The psalm closes with the same words. Each line begins with praise, but in the imperative form. We are told to praise God who dwells "in his sanctuary," God's holy temple in heaven. Then we are told to praise God in "his mighty firmament" or here on earth. In the third line, the command comes to praise God for "mighty deeds."

All the known instruments of the orchestra were included. The priests played the trumpets and the ram's horns. The Levites played the lutes, harps, and cymbals. Young girls and women played the tambourines and danced. Laypeople played the stringed instruments and the pipes. Thus the call to praise God is made to all sections of the community.

Everything that breathes should praise the Lord. Moses told Pharaoh, "'We will go with our young and our old; we will go with our sons and daughters and with our flocks and our herds, because we have the LORD's festival to celebrate'" (Exod. 10:9). So today the tradition continues—all creatures should praise the Lord! Alleluia!

Reflections

❑ Review your day today. As it unfolds, praise God for each element in it. At the end of the day, praise God for all that happened, both good and bad.

❑ Stand up, raise your hands, if possible, dance while you sing a favorite hymn of joy to God.

❑ Write your own version of Psalm 150, and then decorate it with paint or watercolor. Post it somewhere for everyone to see so that they and you can remember to always praise the Lord.

❑ Close your meditation with Psalm 150.

Memory Verse

Let everything that breathes praise the LORD!

(Ps. 150:6)

Acknowledgments *(continued)*

Psalm 1 in meditation 1 is the author's own adaptation and is not to be used or understood as an official translation of the Bible.

All other scriptural quotations used in this book are from the New Revised Standard Version of the Bible. Copyright © 1989 by the Division of Christian Education of the National Council of the Churches of Christ in the United States of America. All rights reserved. Used with permission.

The poem on page 6 is from the *Collected Poems and Plays of Rabindranath Tagore* by Rabindranath Tagore (New York: Collier Books/Macmillan, 1993), page 21. Copyright © 1936 by Macmillan and Company. Reprinted with permission of Simon and Schuster.

The excerpt on page 13 is from *Tales of the Hasidim: The Later Masters*, by Martin Buber (New York: Schocken Books, 1947), page 304. Copyright © 1947 and 1975 by Schocken Books. Used with permission.

The excerpt on page 16 is from *Mekilta De-Rabbi Ishmael*, vol. 2, translated by Jacob Lauterbach (Philadelphia: The Jewish Publication Society of America, 1933), page 277. Copyright © 1933 and 1961 by the Jewish Publication Society of America.

The excerpt on pages 18–19 is from an article by Nancy Fuchs-Kreimer in *Cross Currents*, vol. 42, no. 2 (Summer 1992), pages 212–213. Copyright © 1992 by the Association for Religion and Intellectual Life. Used with permission.

The excerpt on page 23–24 is from *Shabbath*, translated by Rabbi Dr. H. Freedman and edited by Rabbi Dr. I. Epstein, page 127b. (Brooklyn, NY: Soncio Press, n.d.).

The excerpts on pages 25 and 26 are from William Shakespeare's *Hamlet*, edited by M. R. Ridley (New York: Gramercy Books, 1991), page 54. Copyright © 1991 by Outlet Book Company.

The excerpt on page 32 is from *Prayers and Meditations of Saint Anselm,* translated by Sister Benedicta Ward (London: Penguin Classics, 1973) pages 153–156. Copyright © 1973 by Benedicta Ward. Used by permission of the publisher.

The excerpt on page 46 is from *Hasidic Responses to the Holocaust in the Light of Hasidic Thought,* by Pesach Schindler (Hoboken, NJ: Ktav Publishing House, 1990), page 35. Copyright © 1990 by Pesach Schindler.

The Emily Dickinson poem on page 50 is reprinted from *The Poems of Emily Dickinson,* edited by Thomas H. Johnson (Cambridge, MA: The Belknap Press of Harvard University Press). Copyright © 1951, 1955, 1979, 1983 by the President and fellows of Harvard College. Reprinted by permission of the publishers and the Trustees of Amherst College.

The excerpts from "The Death of Ivan Ilych" on page 61 are from *The Raid and Other Stories,* by Leo Tolstoy (Oxford, England: Oxford University Press, 1982), pages 235 and 276. Copyright © 1982 by Oxford University Press.

The excerpt on page 67 is adapted from the *Daily Prayer Book: Ha-Siddur Ha-Shalem,* translated by Philip Birnbaum (New York: Hebrew Publishing Company, 1949), page 16. Copyright © 1947 by Hebrew Publishing Company and copyright © 1977 by Philip Birnbaum.